RAINED OUT AND OTHER TEXAS HOLIDAY DISASTERS

RAINED OUT AND OTHER TEXAS HOLIDAY DISASTERS

COZY MYSTERIES IN A SMALL TOWN WHERE EVERYONE IS HAVING A WORSE HOLIDAY THAN YOU

A BLACK ORCHID ENTERPRISES MYSTERY
BOOK 4

M. R. DIMOND

ISBN: 978-1-956204-13-1

PART ONE

RAINED OUT

CHAPTER 1
MONDAY, THANKSGIVING MINUS 3

Things can always get worse, on Mondays especially. This Monday, the Monday before Thanksgiving, thunder boomed like a timpani audition, accompanied by loud, wooden cracks. Metal shrieked like Godzilla crunching a car while rain continued its artillery fire on majestic Gregg House's galvanized steel roof. Curses went up all around me, in multiple languages, from the fifty-something strangers who'd sought shelter in my home from the floods. Most choked off the bad words because, after all, there were children present, who, on cue, howled as though in the first circle of Hell. (I know Dante named ten circles, but kids should get a break.)

People had brought their pets, as the PSA encouraged them to, and dogs in their crates scattered throughout the 4,000 square feet of house set up a chain of barking. I was tempted to jump in, or rather wade to, my car and drive away, although I knew the rushing water would sweep me away at the first bridge. Being a grown man, almost thirty, a lawyer even, I'm more mature than that, but not so mature I couldn't dream about it. Besides, my business associate Johnny Ly just rang the dinner gong.

Against the flow of stampeding, hungry customers—guests—refugees, I struggled to reach the intake desk. We called it the reception area when the house functioned as Black Orchid Enterprises instead of the City of Beauchamp Emergency Disaster Shelter. I intended to ask the elderly women seated there if they needed mobility assistance or wanted their dinners brought to them. I thought I might gird my loins and ask the same of the workers across the hall in the childcare room, formerly a spare bedroom. Before I got there though, the women had jumped to their feet and joined the tykes and their parents pouring into the long gallery hall in search of food.

Devora Ly, Johnny's grandmother who owned the historical mansion where I now lived and worked, had rounded up her Beauchamp friends and fellow do-gooders to help with the shelter. They needed to evacuate their homes anyway, the area being under flood warning through Thanksgiving. Besides intake and childcare, several of them directed traffic toward the dining room.

At the end of the parent-and-child rush for dinner, another elderly woman emerged from the childcare room. Her long, white hair danced wherever it wanted, and her clothes mashed up Barbie and Hello Kitty in brilliant colors. I'd seen her in the park, training other older women how to use their canes as a singlestick, a fighting style she'd learned in her Regency reenactment club, Austin's Austenites. Their insurance considered whacking people with sticks a better risk than sword fighting with pointed weapons. Her name tag announced her as Marjorie Feral. Since she wrote it herself (complete with hearts over the *j* and *i*), I assumed it was spelled correctly.

She carried a boy of around three or four, not easy when she limped with a cane. I held out my arms for the child.

"JD Thompson, right?" she rasped. She dumped him into my arms. "The lawyer? You'll know what to do."

Though those words always strike fear in my heart, I admitted to my identity. Someone would rat me out if I didn't.

"It's this kid. He doesn't seem to belong to anyone. The others ran off with their parents to eat dinner, but no one came for him."

I peered into the dark brown eyes, big as chalupas. He had a great future as a child model, if he kept those enormous eyes, his clear brown skin, and the rosebud mouth. Some baby product manufacturer would be glad to slap his image on their label.

A loud, nasal voice carried from the front desk. "We'll all have the gluten-free option."

Marjorie snorted, and I looked toward the front door. Three women, formerly with elegant coifs, now just wet hair, must have mistaken the place for a resort.

Mrs. Ly used the voice she acquired while a nurse in Vietnam and then in the Beauchamp School District to correct the impression we were running a vacation center.

I turned my gaze back to the boy. Mrs. Ly must have checked him in, or at least his parents. I took a guess at his language. "Hola, chico."

Marjorie shook her head again. "He doesn't know Spanish. He speaks some indigenous language. One of the helpers—a Guatemalan lady—knew a few words. She asked about his family. He just said, 'not here.' His name is something like Bam Bam."

The boy waved an arm. "Bam."

"Yeah?" I asked.

"Bam!"

Marjorie pinched his chin. "Mrs. Ly gave him a quick physical, like she did everybody, and he seems clean and healthy. What do we do with him?"

I smiled at her. "Thank you, Ms. Feral, for the easiest problem anybody's asked me to solve today."

This Monday's original task had been how to occupy my time with my two partners and housemates taking off for their parents' homes for Thanksgiving and the agencies and courts I deal with shuttered. Not much of a problem.

Then the rain hammered down, unrelenting. Nothing to worry about; rain does fall in Texas sometimes. By late afternoon, emergency weather alerts blared on every device. Johnny and Dianne had returned with reports that the roads were impassible. The city declared a state of emergency and instructed everyone from the low-lying areas of Beauchamp to evacuate to the closest shelter at (1) the Catholic church, (2) the school administration building, or (3) Gregg House.

Decades ago, Mrs. Ly, in her civic-minded fervor, volunteered her 1897 Victorian mansion for a community shelter when needed. She moved into assisted living last year and left the house to her grandson, cat veterinarian Dr. John Ky Ly. He invited his college bandmates (MultiABBA, Texas's multicultural ABBA tribute band—check us out!)

to join him. Accountant Dianne Cortez and I understood the same level of service would be required of us.

I just didn't expect it. Fortunately, earlier in the day, Johnny had picked up his grandmother from her Austin assisted living apartment. With Thanksgiving at his parents' house out of the question because of closed roads, he'd brought her back to Beauchamp, twenty-two miles southeast of Austin and sixty miles north of San Antonio. She had not only prepared for emergencies but knew where everything was.

Looking at the way she and her squad were filling out forms, checking ID, and providing instructions, I was sure she knew where this child belonged. It was just a matter of asking.

I headed in her direction but stopped when Bam Bam stiffened and wailed. I bounced him and whisper-sang a lullaby in his ear (if you call ABBA's "Thank You for the Music" a lullaby, all I could think of in the moment).

"I want to speak to the manager." A platinum-blonde spiritual sister of the previous group raised her voice at Mrs. Ly. She'd also mistaken the house for a Hawaiian spa. She looked like she was moving in. Several rolling suitcases clustered around her, with a three-foot-long duffle bag stacked on top.

Mrs. Ly used her platoon-commanding voice. "As the homeowner, I want to know who is sleeping in my house. Additionally, as a public health nurse with fifty years' experience, I want to know those people are healthy. Communicable diseases spread through shelters like wildfire. I'm doing my best to prevent one from coming in the door. You can, of course, go to another shelter if you don't wish to provide identification or submit to a medical screening."

"The streets are flooded! I was only ten miles from my home when the police turned me back."

Figuring that Mrs. Ly was occupied for the near future, I headed back down the gallery toward the other end of the house, past the buffet tables of food left over from local restaurants who had to close early today and wouldn't reopen until after Thanksgiving. The feast looked devastated already, but I snagged a pizza slice (courtesy of Bobcat Pizza on Main Street) for Bam Bam. He took it and picked at the toppings before dropping them one by one on the floor.

I gave Johnny's dinner gong a light tap and stepped up to the head of the big table. More than fifty faces turned toward me. People murmured how beautiful the boy was. "This child is looking for his lost parents," I announced. "You know how parents wander off. He promises not to be mad if they come back right away."

In case some didn't understand English, I repeated the message in Spanish, which made the native speakers smile behind their hands because I can't roll a Spanish *R* for anything. Even after ten years, Dianne's young cousins find endless amusement in asking me to say *ferrocarril*. The adults in this room didn't laugh out loud, but neither did they respond to my plea.

One of the Spanish speakers said a few words I didn't understand to a young couple whose skin color matched Bam Bam's. Comprehension dawned on their faces, but they didn't claim the child either.

The boy buried his face in my shoulder and sobbed. The seriousness of the situation descended over me like a smothering blanket. I had an unattached, uncommunicative child in a disaster shelter. I looked around the room in panic, searching for help. Dianne's face shone with pure horror. Johnny's was completely blank, like normal. I patted Bam Bam's back in hopes one of us would be comforted.

Mrs. Ly's last combatant, the woman who objected to providing ID, approached the table with a plate of tacos. "Poor little thing. I can look after him. I just love children." She held out her arms. "I'm Candace Dagny. The woman at the front desk can confirm."

She said the last sentence with a sneer, like she intended to hold the grudge throughout her stay.

Everyone looked relieved, a reflection of how I felt. My stomach unknotted. Then either my conscience or law training kicked in, snapping all my body parts back into anxiety. "I appreciate your generosity, ma'am. But because this is my home—that is, shelter—I'm responsible for the child's welfare until we locate his parents or the appropriate organization."

A fortunate, if dripping, distraction came through the back door at that moment. Cacophony erupted with the invasion by Officer Alejandro Quintanilla-Villanueva, Beauchamp's most recent graduate from police academy, and his not-exactly-a-police-dog Cupcake, an insane husky who always looks like she'd savage you for half a dog biscuit. I can confirm. Officer Al stamped his boots on the floor mat in time to the booming thunder while Cupcake danced around him and barked.

Though a good policeman, Officer Al's lack of seniority makes him the town's Officer Friendly, a frequent classroom visitor with Cupcake. Young voices split between "Cupcake!" in adoring tones and screams of terror. When Cupcake, like all long-haired wet dogs, shook herself, adults added disgusted tones to the chorus. Officer Al knelt on the mat and rubbed her with a towel as wet as both of them. Maybe it removed some of the mud.

"Here's someone who can advise us," I said. "Officer Al, we ended up with an extra child, one who doesn't seem to be attached to anyone here. Should you take charge of him?"

Officer Al's pupils grew so big they made his eyes look black, like he'd just returned from the depths of hell. "JD, don't do this to me."

I winced. "Sorry. Didn't mean to."

"I don't have anyone to call, and no one can come get him if you did manage to contact any of the agencies. If this child is warm, fed, dry, and safe, he can stay here with you so I can go deal with those who aren't."

"I accept the charge." I gulped and patted the boy's back. "Can we do anything for you?"

"You can keep Cupcake here while I go back out. I'm on a break, long enough to evacuate my apartment and bring my stuff and Cupcake here. I can't keep her with me in the storm when I'm on duty. I brought her crate, like the PSA said, but she really hates it." He looked down at her sadly.

"So do our dogs," complained a man from further down the table.

A nearby flash of lightning with almost simultaneous thunder made us all blink and jump, including the dogs in their crates. Mournful doggy voices rose in chorus from all over the house. Cupcake took it for a meet-and-greet opportunity and yipped along.

"But if you're not going to be here, she can't be roaming on her own," said Johnny when the noise died down enough for him to be heard.

"Couldn't she stay with you, Johnny?" pleaded Officer Al. "She'll mind you."

Johnny looked alarmed. Dianne and I laughed. The officer took that as a hard no.

Marjorie Feral pulled out her sleeping assignments list and told Officer Al he could set up the crate and his cot in the second-floor recreation area, where the other single men would be sleeping.

Whereas the first floor of Gregg House is a long hallway, wide as an art gallery, with rooms branching off on either side, the second-floor bedrooms cluster around a large open area we call the rec room, where we watch TV and play games.

I could see by their expressions that my partners were having the same vision as I, of Cupcake in a crate in the rec area, available to the general public while on guard duty. This could not end well.

Dianne saved the day. "Officer Alejandro, you and Cupcake can sleep in my room. Darryl too." She looked at our intern, who had moved into the main house from his efficiency apartment in the back yard. "JD and his charge also. I'm sleeping in the cat clinic near my own cat, since she can't be roaming around loose either."

I'd been wondering where all our house cats were. And I was happy to be in a real bedroom. Marjorie had commandeered the other bedrooms, including mine, so that older, disabled, and pregnant people could have a real bed instead of a cot.

"Alrighty then!" exclaimed Darryl Swann, the intern. "That's an upgrade from a cot in the clinic."

I moved directly behind Dianne and murmured into her black, wavy hair, "I hate for you to sleep on a cot in the clinic."

She waited through the next crack of thunder before replying, "It's either that or on the balcony porch, which I don't want to do in this downpour. And sleeping in the guys' dorm hasn't been my fantasy since middle school. Also, put a waterproof sheet under ..." She gestured to the boy in my arms.

Cupcake trotted by, following Officer Al and several men carrying the hated crate. She looked at me and panted in hopes of a treat.

"Bam Bam, meet Cupcake. Nice doggy," I said.

Bam Bam twisted in my arms and screamed. I almost dropped him.

I wondered how sleeping in the same room with the nice doggy was going to go.

The policeman called out, "Everybody who's sleeping on the second floor needs to come meet Cupcake, so she knows who belongs there."

A couple of guys near me snickered.

I patted Cupcake's head and hoped she'd remember me from our past dealings. "Might be a good idea. Once she kept Johnny, Dianne, and me prisoner in our own house. She understands guarding really well. You just have to make sure she's not confused about who or what to guard. See those teeth? They work."

Cupcake grinned, giving us a better look at her weapons of mass destruction.

I was glad she'd be in the crate. It looked strong enough to withstand her powerful jaws.

CHAPTER 2

MONDAY NIGHT, THANKSGIVING MINUS 2.5

After people shuffled off to their own devices, I offered Bam Bam whatever food would fit in his mouth. He just looked at the pizza, egg rolls, hamburgers, tacos, all the finest products of American franchise restaurants. He didn't seem to consider any of it edible. Many would agree with him. Finally, I gave him half a tortilla, which he tore into bits. Some went into his mouth. That was a relief. Tomorrow I'd worry about nutrition.

I followed the largest group of guests down the gallery hall from the kitchen dining area, past the staircase to where a golden velvet sofa and overstuffed chairs of 1940s vintage clustered around a fireplace. Since tonight seemed like a good time to veg out in front of family-friendly TV, someone had exposed the large TV on the opposite wall that normally hides behind a gold and red silk Vietnamese wall hanging. People shoved the chairs into a line of sight with the TV while they argued about which movie would appeal to all ages. Adding to that noise, louder than the weather for once, Mrs. Ly and her friends in the reception area still welcomed new people, increasingly wetter and bedraggled.

Viewing options were limited because current internet service ranged from spotty to none. That left the library of DVDs from long ago, nothing later than Johnny's childhood. Despite teenage groans, the debate narrowed to *Fraggle Rock* versus *Care Bears*, in deference to the young ears and eyes. My mental state had degraded to the point where either was fine with me, but before I could plop myself and Bam Bam in front of the screen, my partners and intern came to collect me.

I didn't think we were having a band rehearsal, though we could have, and it would have been more entertaining. Instead, Dianne herded us back to the dining table at the far end of the gallery, almost to the horizon. The kitchen, suitable for a chef, sprawled on one side of the table and a baby grand piano on the other. Two teenage girls pounded out "Heart and Soul" with the verve and power of dock workers. I'd have sworn they were using their fists.

Dianne (alto, choreographer) announced, "We need to take inventory."

"Of what?" I (bass-baritone, keyboards) asked.

"Food," said Johnny (tenor, bass guitar). "I'm not sure we have enough for this many people. I know we all went to the store today, but many of the shelves were bare."

"Right. Picked over for the double disaster of holiday and flood," affirmed Darryl (substitute soprano singing in falsetto). Our band leader and regular soprano, the only one of us trying to make a career of music, was traveling in East Texas when the rains hit. "Of course, Mrs. Ly already had a big supply of nonperishable emergency rations. I can live indefinitely on Vienna sausages and ramen."

The rest of us viewed that as a threat and hit the kitchen in search of alternatives. You'd think a house with two refrigerators in the kitchen and one on the back porch and a double-door walk-in pantry would be already stuffed with food, but for weeks we'd been eating with the goal of clearing out food storage space. None of us had planned to be in town for Thanksgiving, and Johnny intended to start holiday cooking in December. Our shelves didn't look much better than the stores we'd raided this afternoon.

Our final inventory led off with two turkeys, almost forty pounds each—the only ones left in the grocery store—and the Tofurky roast Johnny bought. Maybe the gluten-free brigade would share it with him. Then followed more restaurant donations and bits of this and that, not to mention the ramen and canned meat. We hoped to eke out meals by combining them until we could get the turkeys cooked, which would provide multiple meals for everyone.

The list ended with ingredients to make tamales—masa harina, pork loin, chili peppers, and corn husks—that Dianne refused to let anyone touch, because if she couldn't go home for Thanksgiving, she was making tamales like her grandmother always made.

My eyes narrowed. The last time Dianne cooked tamales, to my knowledge, was ten years ago when we were dating. And like me, she calculated her holiday trips home to spend as little time there as possible.

She beckoned us back to the heavy wood dining table where she pulled out her laptop, the better to develop one of her dreaded spreadsheets. "Johnny doesn't want to turn strangers loose in the kitchen, so we'll each take a supervisory shift for meals. Darryl will assist, when needed, and our guests can help."

I leaned back to balance my chair on two legs. "This not being a resort and spa."

She continued, "Johnny's in charge of dinners, I'll do lunches, and JD, you do breakfast."

I nodded. It is a truth universally acknowledged that my culinary repertoire consists of pancakes and grilled cheese sandwiches, not usually in the same meal.

"We'll all work on Thanksgiving dinner. JD, you'll cook the turkeys."

My chair crashed back down on four legs. "What? Why?" I demanded.

"Because I'm making tamales. Johnny's making the vegetables, all of them, with Darryl's help, and he's never cooked meat. And won't."

My vocal pitch rose in panic. "I don't know how to cook a turkey! I don't even know what to do first!"

"Thaw them," volunteered Darryl. "The grannies said to soak them in water, but I think those turkeys are ostriches. They're too big for the kitchen sink. I put them in Dianne's bathtub."

"What were you doing in my bathroom?" she exclaimed.

He shrugged. "You told me to make sure all the bathrooms had supplies. We do. Mrs. Ly had plenty of toilet paper in her emergency stash."

Everyone's expressions lightened. We hadn't been able to find many paper products on our shopping trips.

Darryl continued, "I scouted out the best place for turkey thawing, and your deep, long luxury tub is the only one that will hold both of them. Should I turn on the jets?"

"You should go get those turkeys and put them, put them ..." Dianne's voice rose toward the high end of her chocolatey contralto range.

"How about we put them in the efficiency apartments out back?" I interrupted.

Behind the house stood Johnny's grandfather's octagonal meditation building. To its left was a strip of four efficiency apartments, one occupied by Darryl as part of his salary, though he'd now evacuated to higher ground in the main house. The other three were vacant. To the right was a barn, formerly a garage, now converted to a cat habitat by the local Boy Scouts for Beauchamp's new assistant animal control officer, Johnny. He'd brought the shelter cats into his clinic on the north side of the house earlier in the afternoon.

Johnny looked at each of us, baffled. "You're not thinking of soaking the turkeys in room-temperature water from Monday to Thursday, are you? The resulting bacteria could make people sick."

"Really?" I asked. "You're the science officer, but I have memories of turkeys soaking in the sink at holiday time."

"My granny's been thawing turkeys that way all her life," agreed Darryl, rising to his feet. "Worked fine, except when the cat got them. I'll take them to the apartments out back. The birds are so big they'll have to go in separate refrigerators. And, JD, there's this thing called Google I can show you. It has recipes and other stuff."

I scowled. "I'm not even ten years older than you. Google got me through school. If we ever get connectivity for longer than a minute, I'm sure I can find a recipe."

I was going to help with the turkey transfer, but Bam Bam fastened his arms around my neck and wouldn't let go. I didn't want to drag him out into the rain, so I let Darryl handle the turkeys.

It felt like bedtime to me, though I was ten the last time I went to bed before double digits. Bam Bam's yawn and drooping eyelids gave me hope that he agreed. We made it past the screens around Cupcake's crate with no reaction from the child and just a weak whine from the dog. Having armed myself with doggy treats, I flipped one over the top of the screen and into the crate. That was enough to keep her quiet.

Bam Bam objected to the cardboard crib that was part of Gregg House's disaster supplies, so I settled him beside me on Dianne's California king-size bed on the waterproof sheets from the crib. I planned to fiddle with my phone while he slept, but I might have fallen asleep before he did.

In the stupid hours of the morning, Cupcake roared in full guard-dog mode. I jumped up with a shout. Bam Bam screamed when I flipped on the light. On the far side of the bed, Darryl moaned, and I pushed Bam Bam toward him. I sent Officer Al an SOS text before heading out into the second-floor rec room with my heart pounding loud as the rain.

I opened the door to chaos. Men on couches or cots shouted. They struggled out of their blankets and waved their phones for light, creating quite a show. I flipped on the room's overhead light.

Seven men, ages twenty to forty, blinked. I stepped around the furniture to make sure no one was hiding.

I demanded, "Did you hear anything?"

"The dog."

"Before the dog," I clarified.

"What's wrong with the dog?"

I squinted at the room. "She detected something—someone—she considered a threat. Did any of you approach her?"

They were insulted. "We're sleeping, man. Could be someone going upstairs to the attic."

I looked toward the stairs on the other side of the room from Dianne's door. "Nope. They set up her crate as far from the stairs as possible. Besides, we'd have heard the footsteps.

From the ring of bedrooms around the social area, elderly folks who rated a bed appeared in the doorways. The women held their canes like weapons, some of Marjorie's students, no doubt. Over their demands for answers, I repeated what I'd said to the men and asked whether anyone had come into the hall. Cupcake had been introduced to everyone who had a right to be here, so the "No" answers didn't surprise me.

Everyone looked to be in a groggy, just-awakened state. I didn't think an intruder could have hidden in a bedroom or bathroom after people started to wake up, but I checked anyway.

The only other place to hide was the closet under the stairs. I threw open the door and jumped back when I saw four shadowy figures in the dark.

I flipped the closet light, but it was burned out, an odd thing in a house furnished with LED long-lasting bulbs. The light from the outer room was enough for me to identify the life-size cardboard photo cutouts of Multi-ABBA. The room was stuffed full of costumes, promo stuff, and supplies, so I didn't look any further. I returned to the still screaming child.

Officer Al thundered up the stairs, louder than the rain clattering on the roof. He panted louder than Cupcake while he tried to soothe her. I updated him on what I knew: practically nothing.

"Somebody was here, somebody who shouldn't have been." He frowned. "JD, you've got a house full of strangers. You need security, somebody patrolling through the night. I can take a two-hour shift, but you need more than me."

Bam Bam still whimpered, so I held him close. I said to Officer Al, "You get a few hours rest. No one's going to sleep with him crying, so I'll take the first shift.

Remembering the long nights my mother walked with my colicky sisters, I hoped to put Bam Bam to sleep the same way. He settled into long, steady sobs as I sang "Move On," a nice slow, soft song in triple time. I didn't think we'd disturb anyone because the storm kicked into high gear. The wind shrieked at high volume, thunder boomed, and lightning flashed close by. The guest dogs whined in their crates spread over both floors, attic, and basement.

I was wrong about not disturbing anyone. Bam Bam and I reached the bottom of the stairs when Dianne stepped out of the clinic, her golden Siamese cat Nevada blinking in rage in her arms.

"Madre de Dios, JD, what is going on? Why was Cupcake barking?"

I bounced Bam Bam while I explained. Her terra cotta skin flushed in anger at the thought of someone prowling the place at night, though she at least was safe behind the locked clinic door. I intended to lock the bedroom door if Bam Bam ever shut up and we could go back to bed.

"Darryl's patrolling after me, then Officer Al. That will get us close to dawn. We'll set up an official security team and schedule tomorrow."

Scratching her cat's head, Dianne nodded. "Johnny always gets up early. I'll let him know. I can take a shift too. And you and I can switch meals tomorrow. I'll do breakfast, and you can do lunch." She placed Bam Bam's hand on Nevada's forehead. "Nice kitty, yes?"

Bam Bam interrupted his tears to explore the soft fur. The cat glared at the child.

Dianne's lovely face looked pinched and drawn. Exhaustion? Disappointment? I was going to ask, but what came out of my mouth was something more familiar. "How's Johnny doing?"

During our sophomore year of college, Johnny moved into Casa Cortez, a ramshackle old mansion in Austin, with us and eight other friends. He lived in the garage apartment and joined us in the big house to prepare meals, one of his stress-coping strategies. He agreed to one half-hour of socializing each month, not hard when we had parties at least that often.

Dianne looked thoughtful. "He loves serving the community—"

"He wouldn't be assistant justice of the peace and assistant animal control officer if he didn't."

"—People, not so much. Especially more than fifty of them under his own roof."

"True."

Dianne shrugged. "He'll be okay tomorrow if he divides the day between the clinic, taking care of our cats, the shelter cats, and every-body's pets that they brought, and the kitchen."

"And you?"

"I'm fine." She cuddled her cat close and backed into the clinic.

As I continued my walk with "Move On" and its appropriate watery imagery, she harmonized as she shut the clinic door.

CHAPTER 3

TUESDAY, THANKSGIVING MINUS 2

I could have used another few hours sleep the next morning, but when you have a toddler, you wake with the toddler. I staggered downstairs carrying him on my hip. I stopped short of the kitchen and closed my eyes in pain.

I found Dianne in charge of breakfast, as promised, meaning it must be her fault. Cats jumped on every surface as they fought each other for anything worth eating. Hands on hips, she yelled at Darryl for letting them escape the clinic. He shouted back that he couldn't help it. Our guests shouted about the disruption. Children shouted because all the adults did. They chased the cats with delighted cries of "Kitty!" and offered food that the cats hadn't yet stepped on.

I plowed my way through the kitchen to the walk-in pantry. "Dianne, grab your own cat. Darryl, get ready to play zone defense."

From the pantry, I grabbed a bag of cat treats and shook it like maracas. That got the attention of the four Gregg House cats, known as the Very Good Kitties. They darted toward me and climbed my legs. I was glad for heavy jeans. The visiting cats, also curious, came my way with Darryl's encouragement of waving his arms to the tune of "Shoo, kitty, kitty, kitty."

I managed to get the bag open, even with Bam Bam in one arm. I pitched a spray of treats into the pantry. I repeated as necessary until all cats were squabbling inside. Darryl and I shut the door and leaned against it. I might have looked triumphant.

"Okay, genius. Now what?" Dianne struggled with her own squalling cat, a beautiful flame point Siamese trying to fold into a Mobius strip.

Guessing that Nevada was furious because all the other cats got all the treats in the universe and starvation was imminent, I strolled over and held out a few treats in my hand. Her tail lashed Dianne's face one last time. Nevada gobbled the treats while grumbling.

I offered another handful of treats. "Now we extract them one at a time."

"I'm gonna put on my rubber cat-handling suit." Darryl left his post by the pantry doors and headed for the clinic.

I scooted back to the pantry when the doors shook from enraged cats on the other side. I smiled while the chorus of crashing food cans, packages, and squealing, growling cats crescendoed.

"What's going on?" a woman's voice demanded, the type of elderly voice that took me back to childhood and promised punishment.

In full rain gear, Mrs. Ly stood at the kitchen entrance. Even peeking out of a voluminous rain poncho, her face looked fierce. She's always scared me, even after years' acquaintance, when I'd learned that her demeanor came from being a tiny Jewish woman who'd dealt with soldiers and rotten kids under the worst circumstances.

Officer Al stood behind her with her overnight bag and medical bag.

Johnny burst out of the clinic door on the opposite side of the room. "I got your text, Grandmother. Don't go." Darryl followed close behind, in full cat protection.

Officer Al winced. "The other shelters don't have any medical personnel, and we can't bring anybody in from out of town."

I glanced out the windows into the pouring rain, which told me nothing I didn't know. A crack of thunder boomed and seconds later, the snap of a large tree limb. I peered out the window again but couldn't tell which tree had been struck.

Johnny's Adam's apple quivered. "I'll go."

"No!" exclaimed Darryl and Dianne together. Darryl added, "Who's gonna corral these cats? Not to mention dogs."

"You're a vet, Johnny," explained Officer Al, as though Johnny had forgotten.

"I've had first aid training. My grandmother deserves a rest at her …" he swallowed. "… age. Grandmother, the rabbis would say you do not have to complete the work, especially when you've never abstained from it."

She glared when he uttered the A word. "And my Methodist friends would say 'Do all the good you can, at all the times you can, to all the people you can, as long as ever you can.' Today I can, and I will."

She stomped out the back door and pulled up short at the steps. Officer Al, with an apologetic glance at Johnny, ran after her. After a brief discussion, he descended the steps and waited as she climbed on his back with her legs straight out in front. With her bags banging against his sides, he set off at a staggering gallop for his massive all-terrain vehicle. He nearly went down when Mrs. Ly twisted to shout something back at the house.

A glance at the expressions in the room told me nobody understood her, but Dianne smiled and waved. I waved Bam Bam's hand. Johnny jerked his hand up in a spasmodic wave as he bowed his head.

In a smaller voice higher than his usual tenor, Johnny said, "My dad's going to kill me, not to mention my Aunt Chana."

Johnny went to assist Darryl in removing the cats from the pantry. Their competence bored the guests still at the breakfast table. The women turned to the next source of interest, the beautiful boy in my arms.

As they cooed and patted him, I searched through the remaining donuts and other breakfast pastries donated by the local donut shop. I grabbed a few sausage-cheese kolaches for myself and offered Balam a donut hole.

He stared at it with that universal child expression that meant "You've got to be kidding me."

I'd never seen it inspired by donuts. I offered him my kolache, but he wasn't any more interested. He began his soft wail, the one I'd already learned could go on for hours. I looked around in panic. Dianne, in the midst of cleanup in the wake of the feline marauders, shrugged her shoulders.

I was running options through my mind when the Guatemalan lady left her husband and two girls at the table and approached me. She handed me a small box, like a single-serving of cereal. The label read *incaparina*. If I understood the label correctly, the contents of the box contained ground corn and soy.

I smiled back and asked, "How do I serve it?" I dumped it into a bowl and mimed pouring something else in. I couldn't imagine handing the kid a bowl of powdered grains. I pointed to various choices, and she picked maple syrup. She mixed in just enough to make a mush.

Bam Bam showed himself willing and able to feed himself when there was something worth eating. She and I exchanged grateful, relieved smiles.

The murmur of voices around me ebbed and flowed like gibberish. Suddenly, real words hit my ears.

"I wonder why that family doesn't claim their child. He's obviously hers—looks just like her."

"Maybe it's not the husband's child, and he won't let her take it back."

I whipped around, trying to find the speakers, but the words evaporated and I saw nothing but pleasant faces blithering about the weather.

Dianne stood straight and stiff by the stove.

"You heard?" I whispered.

She snapped a nod at me while she searched the nearby faces. We both looked at Bam Bam, who looked nothing like the Guatemalan woman except for dark hair and eyes.

She, who wouldn't have understood the words if she had heard them, rooted around in her shoulder bag. With another smile, she handed me several more cereal boxes before returning to her own family. Donut frosting of many colors decorated her children's faces like makeup, so I didn't worry that Bam Bam was depriving them. Good to know they were getting used to their new country.

Johnny joined us and started tense negotiations with Dianne over use of the oven.

"But I'll need it to prepare lunch in an hour," I protested over their undertones.

"That's why you're serving sandwiches," snapped Dianne.

Bam Bam finished eating his cereal and had moved on to the artistic phase of eating: painting himself and the highchair tray. I hated to choke off his creativity, but maple syrup is sticky, and he was covering every reachable surface.

I was caught in a never-ending cycle of wipe one hand, wipe the other while the clean hand went back into the mess. There was always more mess, even when I thought I'd cleaned it up. A Latino of my own age stepped in to help. His experience with three small daughters had taught him a few tricks, he said. Between us, we soon had the boy clean enough until I could get him into the bathtub.

"He is a beautiful boy," said my helper, Matías, who pinched the boy's mostly clean cheek. "Do you know what will happen to him?"

"I'm hoping he can return to his family, wherever they are," I replied.

"That is your first priority?"

"Yes, of course," I said.

Matías masked his emotions into a blank expression worthy of Johnny. "I've heard that migrant children without families are adopted out to white families, like the woman at dinner who wanted him." He wrinkled his nose like he smelled something bad.

"They don't when I'm involved, and I'm staying involved until Bam Bam is settled, preferably with his parents." My brow furrowed. I hoped the rains hadn't carried his family away. We wouldn't know the extent of the tragedies for weeks.

Matías's face relaxed. "If you can't find his parents, please let me know if he needs a home, even a temporary one. My wife and I have three beautiful girls, but we would like a boy too. Our culture would be closer to his than other options."

"It's too early to make any plans," I said, like I was addressing a jury. I wasn't about to explain the intricacies of Texas immigration policies. "I'll let you know how things progress. I don't know what

Guatemala does, but in the U.S., indigenous children are placed with indigenous families when possible."

Matías looked relieved. "Certainly the next best, if you can't locate his people."

We exchanged pleasant farewells. I lifted the kid out of the high chair and headed toward the stairs, where Candace and the gluten-free crowd gathered. Candace stepped forward to accost me.

"I'm positive there's illegal immigrants here," she stage whispered. "You should tell that policeman so he can arrest them. That old lady who owns the house should know which ones. She made copies of all our IDs. Unless they have fake ones, of course."

Many responses hovered on the tip of my tongue, none of them advisable. I settled for, "Do you know what I do for a living?"

"You're a lawyer," she stated. "So you're officially part of law enforcement, right?"

I ground my teeth. "I'm an immigration lawyer. It's not my job to harass anyone who's sought shelter from the storms, and Mrs. Ly and Officer Quintanilla-Villanueva would agree." Warming to my theme, my voice rose in pitch and volume. "The roads are impassable. Food is uncertain. The storm doesn't show any signs of stopping. Law enforcement's just trying to keep people safe, whether by rescue or stopping those bent on harm."

She took a step back, her eyes wide with alarm. I judged it the right moment to mount the stairs, holding the child close, though he didn't understand the words being slung around.

One of the gluten-free ladies called after me, "I've heard that you can go to the immigration centers and adopt a child who doesn't have a parent with him. Is that true?"

That stopped me in my tracks. I held my breath to keep from spitting out my opinions. I settled on, "No," and continued up the stairs.

I let off steam by helping Bam Bam splash huge waves in Dianne's luxury tub. Post-bath, with Bam Bam enveloped in one of my T-shirts, I ducked past the living room TV (now showing a *Mr. Rogers* episode) and headed, determined, for my first-floor office.

Bam Bam in his voluminous top garnered some startled looks. A mother who looked too young to be leading around the strawberry-blonde toddler beside her waylaid me before I could reach my office. I tensed up, expecting another offer to adopt the boy, but instead she offered me some of her daughter's spare clothes, if Bam Bam and I didn't mind Strawberry Shortcake.

"I didn't think there would be a washing machine, so I brought as much as I could. Kids get filthy so fast, don't they? But everything Aria has is Strawberry Shortcake, her absolute favorite."

Aria hugged her Strawberry Shortcake doll and beamed up at me. She pointed at the boy and said, "Bam Bam." He waved at her. They must have met each other yesterday in the kids' room.

I expressed fervent gratitude for all raiment, even pink underpants covered with strawberries and a similar ruffled nightgown. If I could sing onstage in a rainbow-striped satin suit, Bam Bam could survive a few days of girly clothes. I promised Aria's mother she could use the washing machine whenever she needed it.

In my office in the south turret, I settled Bam Bam on the floor with some fidget toys my sisters gave me for my birthday—still not sure why they thought I needed a twisty dinosaur and a popper square—while I combed through my list of immigration contacts. With the chaotic weather, sometimes I could get a call through, sometimes not. Any call that connected went right to voicemail with a message that they were closed for the holiday and the flood. Eventually I started in on those top-secret, emergency-only cell phone numbers, and reached Teresa Monroy of Los Anfitriones.

Los Anfitriones means welcomers, greeters, hosts, something like that. A nonprofit group, they do their best to advocate for recent immigrants to Texas, mostly from Mexico and points south. When they need legal advocacy, they call me. Otherwise, they're a constant presence at both child and adult immigration holding centers. They make life as good as they can for the inmates and hustle cases along in hopes of liberty and justice for all. Teresa often deals with the children's facility in Fort Walter, thirty minutes from Beauchamp, where children are separated from their parents for reasons I'll never understand.

She greeted me with typical holiday cheer. "What do you think I can do for you or anybody else when the roads are flooded out and every employee snuck out early on Monday?"

"I'm not asking what you can do for me, but what I can do for you." I explained Bam Bam's appearance. "We were thinking that his parents lived nearby. Maybe they dropped him off while they went home to get other people or supplies, but the local Guatemalans don't know him. Local authorities aren't much help. They're still pulling people out of the river and off of roofs. So I'm casting my net wider, to you, in effect."

She turned thoughtful. "An extra child. Not something you see every day. Let me call around. Send me photos if you can."

I felt better for having someone else working on the problem, since I was confined to cleaning and feeding the boy and trying to keep the shelter from descending into Lord of the Flies. I sent Teresa photos that tried to exclude girlish cartoon characters.

Almost jubilant, I returned to the kitchen. Dianne had set up a spreadsheet for oven usage, and she told me I could bake cornbread now or never. No, Johnny would not do it for me, she said. Johnny was preparing ten dishes already.

Johnny glanced at me while he checked his current casserole in the oven. "About ten minutes more. Then you can raise the temperature to cook your cornbread."

I set Bam Bam in a high chair, close to the kitchen island where I'd be working. He still had the dinosaur twisty-fidget and the popper-bubble square. He alternated between poking them and chewing on them. "We need to search the security tapes and pull stills of everyone here. Teresa at Los Anfitriones is checking with immigration centers to see if they're missing a kid. I sent her Bam Bam's photo. Since I'm baking cornbread, ready or not, do you want to look through the security tapes, Johnny?"

Johnny's face brightened, no doubt at the thought of sitting in his clinic office by himself and twentyish disgruntled felines. He'd get to spend hours viewing security tapes to the music of their howls. He plowed through the surrounding crowd with a spring in his step.

Someone had marked the eggs with a wax crayon to indicate which person or dish had claimed them. I grabbed two marked "pancakes," since I was the official pancake maker. I'd apologize to myself in the morning and hope for forgiveness. Then I had a brief altercation with Dianne over who was going to use the mixer.

She brandished the mixer like a weapon. "If I don't mix the masa dough long enough, my tamales will fall apart!"

I held up my hands in surrender and backed away from the beaters. "Okay, I'll go on manual." I picked up a fork and beat eggs and milk into the cornbread mix while I sang "On and On and On." It has the perfect beat for the job.

By this time, my lunch troops were milling about, and I instructed them to put out anything that could go in a sandwich. People could assemble their own. I felt they stretched a point in some cases, but who was I to judge what anyone would stuff between two slices of bread? All that mattered was that we had one more heap of edible material we could call a meal. My hope was that we could make it until Thursday, when we would have seventy-five to eighty pounds of cooked turkey that we could eat through the weekend.

I glanced out the back windows at the never-ending rain, the water line creeping ever closer to the backyard buildings. I wasn't worried about water getting in the house—Gregg House is the highest point in a flat town—but I was worried that no one could ever leave. Conversely, no one could get in to claim Bam Bam either, except by boat or all-weather terrain vehicles like the police had.

I pulled my aromatic loaves from the oven. Then I had to fight off demands to serve it right then.

Using my elbows to push back the crowd, I yelled, "This is for Thursday's stuffing!"

The crowd fell back in disappointment. I felt triumphant, but then Bam Bam held out his hand. He was willing to eat as much as I'd give him, which turned out to be as much as he demanded. My Thanksgiving stuffing was going to fit in a finger bowl.

Later in the day we established the security team. Thinking of liability issues, I made only one stipulation: No loaded guns. Marjorie and her elderly students pulled their lips back in feral smiles and twisted their canes in their hands.

I handed Officer Al the schedule and uniform when he returned after work.

"Rainbow satin vests decorated with glow-in-the-dark paint?" he gobbled.

"From one of MultiABBA's stage outfits. People thought their security officer status should be apparent at a glance."

He continued to look aghast, so I told him he could wear Dianne's rainbow satin headband around his arm instead.

I also told him about my call to Teresa of Los Anfitriones. "Did the Beauchamp police rescue anybody today who's looking for a lost boy?"

"No. But we won't hear about everybody who needs help, much less rescue them. It'll take weeks to account for everybody." His expression sagged. This disaster was his first as a policeman. I hated to think what he must be seeing.

"I still think the most likely explanation is that someone dropped him off, intending to come right back, and couldn't for some reason." The weight in my voice matched his. The story was unlikely to have a happy ending.

I took the first security shift, bouncing Bam Bam down the hall to the set we sang at MultiABBA's last gig. Since I was singing my bass back-up part, it bored Bam Bam to sleep fast.

That night the rain slacked off from an artillery attack to a low grumble. I could hear Cupcake's claws tapping the wooden floor while she walked beside Officer Al on their rounds and, later, the uneven steps and thumps of cane-wielding senior citizens. Maybe tomorrow I'd be able to see the sky and hear myself think.

CHAPTER 4
WEDNESDAY, THANKSGIVING MINUS 1

The storm stopped by the time we woke on Wednesday. I took Bam Bam on the back porch to check the water levels and discovered that the storm stopping didn't mean the rain wasn't falling. It still came down steadily, but now stealthily, not disturbing the metal roof or whipping through the trees.

The water hadn't crept any closer, giving me faint hope that things would get better from this point. The cars were safe. The barn shelter was safe. The meditation building was safe. The water hadn't invaded the row of apartments, but a massive tree branch had fallen over one end, but not on Darryl's apartment, I was glad to see.

At that moment, a bobcat, mouth full, trotted around the side of the apartment building. No doubt she had been a good bobcat, because the heavens had blessed her with a huge bald turkey. The plastic wrap had been no challenge. She was probably grateful not to have to wash and defeather the bird she hadn't had to chase.

"Hey, you! That's our dinner!" I half-shouted, trying to control the noise and violence because I had a toddler in my arms. I grabbed a set of tongs from the grill and banged them on the grate. I wish I could say I remembered Johnny's instructions about making noise to chase away a bobcat, but I just wanted her to drop her prize. I didn't consider whether we wanted to eat something a bobcat had chewed on first.

Unimpressed, she didn't quite roll her eyes at me. She turned and padded away, probably to feed her teenage kittens. I thought I'd be older before I started yelling, "Get off my lawn." I also thought I'd be yelling it at people. She flipped up her little tail to show me the white underside. I interpreted that gesture as the bobcat middle finger.

A good percentage of the current house occupants lined up along the windows that cover the back of the house. Some, including my housemates, spilled out onto the porch with me.

"There's a bobcat in my apartment?" Darryl shrieked.

"No, she was in the one on the opposite end. But I want to get the other turkey out, if it's still there, in case she comes back." I started for the steps until I remembered the child I was holding. I have no parenting expertise, but I imagine you don't take your child with you to stalk wild animals.

Not that I knew how to do that anyway, but Johnny did, having completed most of a zoo vet residency. He set off for the apartments with his catch pole, in case the bobcat had invited her friends.

"So, Darryl," I said in casual tones. "How do you think the bobcat opened the refrigerator?"

He traced a pattern on the floor with one shoe. "I guess this is going to come out, one way or another."

"The turkey sure did."

"I put one turkey in my fridge. Had to take out all the shelves to do it, but it's not like I had much in there anyway. I was supposed to spend the week at my grandmother's house."

We sighed over lost plans. Both my sisters, my grandparents, and even my father sent messages for me to stay put until the roads were safe. I'd replied that I was running a disaster shelter and had no idea when I'd be able to go anywhere. It's not like I'd leave my friends in the lurch.

Refocusing, I asked, "And the other turkey?"

"Have you ever been in the other apartments? No one's lived in any of them in forever, and the places are gross. The fridges looked like a science experiment from Frankenstein's lab. It was easier to clean the bathtub—also gross—and put the turkey there. But I filled the tub to the top with water. The turkey was submerged." His eyes pleaded with me.

That would carry no weight with Johnny, invading bacteria, or court of law, if someone sued us over food poisoning. However—I looked out where I'd last seen the bobcat. "Darryl, this is one of those points we call moot. No, you shouldn't have done it, but the bobcat solved the problem. Now the problem is what are we going to eat this weekend, but there's no sense in crying over stolen turkeys."

"I'm not fired?"

"Not yet."

Soon Johnny returned with the other turkey but no additional wildlife. With the excitement over, the crowd began to disperse. They fled faster when he said we had to do something about the tree branch and the hole in the apartment roof, even in the rain.

"Put a tarp over it," I suggested. "I bought one the other day at Big Tex from their seasonal display."

Johnny's eyes widened. A native of land-locked San Antonio, he had no concept of wet weather disasters. "Why?"

"Because you buy tarps during rainy disasters," I replied. "And Pop-Tarts, beer, and masking tape."

Johnny made a face. "I saw the beer you bought. No one would drink that sewer water."

And my Pop-Tart substitute was some kind of processed breakfast pastry on a flat surface, maybe cardboard. By the time the pantry was empty, it might taste pretty good though.

Johnny offered his special craft brew beer and the first pieces of his next pies to anyone volunteering for Team Tarp. That offer brought out several construction workers, who set out for the apartment building. Johnny brought out the pumpkins and got to work, turning the kitchen island into a pumpkin crime scene, full of rinds and guts.

I left Bam Bam to his breakfast of corn-soy mush and tangerine bits while I mourned over the remaining turkey. Still frozen, but no bite marks. Would we have enough for everyone? Maybe, if some people ate Johnny's Tofurky, but the bobcat had eliminated the leftovers we were counting on.

"I could make my grandmother's recipe for dill pickle soup," Johnny mused. "It's an old Jewish tradition. It could stretch a few meals."

Because no one would eat it, I thought. Dianne and I locked horrified gazes, in a mutual pact to starve before we'd eat pickle soup. She forced her voice into neutral tones. "Let's see what we have after the Thanksgiving meal."

Johnny agreed. "I'm not sure we have enough yogurt for soup."

I consulted my phone and cheered when I found an internet connection. Google said it would take several more days to completely thaw the bird, but I could cook it frozen by adding half again as much cooking time. I'd better get it in the oven if we wanted it done before Christmas.

Dianne had other ideas. "Johnny's making pies and cranberry sauce, and I'm making tamales after that. Look at the spreadsheet. The oven won't be free until after tonight's dinner."

"When am I supposed to roast this buzzard?" I demanded.

"It's your fault for not buying ready-made pies and canned cranberry sauce!" she snapped.

"There weren't any! The broken supply chain during a combined disaster and holiday is my fault?"

We were squared off, ready to shout down the rafters when Marjorie Feral, clad in her own Strawberry Shortcake sheath, walked between us. "What we did at my house, with the whole family trying to cook at once, is put the turkey in the oven at night after everyone went to bed. You adjust the oven temperature down so the bird doesn't dry out. Then you brown it the next day right before the meal."

I eyed Dianne and offered a truce. "I'll do that if you'll do the math."

She raised an elegant eyebrow. "Math?"

"Word problem: To cook a forty-pound, half-frozen turkey overnight to be ready whenever you want to eat it tomorrow, how long should it cook and at what temperature? Meanwhile, I want to test something."

To the accompaniment of Johnny chopping pumpkins, I silently thanked Mrs. Ly for buying a super-jumbo extra-large foil roasting pan when she bought the turkeys. Even so, more than half the turkey stuck out over the top when I placed it in the pan. Biggest muffin top ever. Maybe when I covered it in foil the juices wouldn't leak out.

That might have been too hopeful, but I would never know. I opened the oven door to cries from whoever was cooking what, and tried to wedge the pan in on the edge of the bottom shelf. I frowned. No way could I push the whole bird into the oven, not with the breastbone and legs sticking up in the air.

I set the pan and turkey on the counter and retreated to the dining room table, out of everyone's way. Johnny whacked the pumpkins louder than ever, which suited my mood. What were we going to eat, if I couldn't get the main course in the oven? Fake Pop-Tarts?

Johnny walked by me with a pumpkin under his arm, the green and orange–striped one I bought because it was so bright and merry. He went into the backyard without speaking. I couldn't imagine what he was doing. I turned to the window to watch, after handing Bam Bam a cracker.

Johnny stood by the woodpile, adjusting his safety glasses. The pumpkin sat on the block we used to chop firewood to size. He brought the axe down in one sleek, swift motion. Instead of dividing the gourd into two equal pieces with a clean cut, the pumpkin shattered.

He squatted to study the pieces and picked up a few to bring into the house. After drying himself off, he set the pieces on the table in front of me. "That pumpkin was a varnished gourd. Decorative, not meant to be eaten. In fact, inedible."

I winced. "So, for dessert, we have—"

He held up a finger and counted off. "(1) and (2) Two pies made from the other pumpkins, assuming they come out acceptably. (3) From Grandmother's and my shopping trip, a strawberry-rhubarb pie, broken into several pieces. (4) From your shopping trip, broken sugar cookies."

"By my calculations—"

"We're still short. Even if we had any more ingredients, I wouldn't have time to make anything." Johnny's voice tightened like a piano string.

Dianne joined us. "Madre de Dios, Johnny, just put all the available fruit in a pan, add half your weight in sugar, sprinkle the cookies on top, and cook it to mush. Call it a cobbler or clafouti. People never complain about dessert if you add enough sugar."

Johnny looked ill. Raised in his Vietnamese grandfather's restaurant, he thinks there's one correct way to prepare any dish. Dianne, eldest in a large family and frequently in charge of younger and hungry children, mixes handfuls of the nearest ingredients with all the artistry of a rabid raccoon.

And yet … I narrowed my eyes. Here she was making exact measurements for her tamales, preparing them like her grandmother taught her and cooking them a precise amount of time. So what the actual—

My phone rang. When I saw the caller ID, I scooped up Bam Bam and ran to my office. I didn't bother to shut the door.

Teresa didn't waste words. "Monday was crazy at the children's immigration center. So many new arrivals."

I swallowed. That translated into separated families. "Is everyone safe?"

"Everyone except a three-year-old boy who disappeared. His father, you can imagine, is frantic. "

"I can. I sent you his photo, right? He's right here, eating sugar cookie bits."

"You did, and that's him. Balam Caal. He was separated from his father and taken to the children's center, but until now, no one could find him. If the water keeps receding, the roads should be passable tomorrow. If that's true, I'll bring Adelmo Caal to your place."

"Please do. I'll keep him right beside me, just like I've been doing, until I can hand him over to his father."

"You do that. The center people recognized a platinum blonde woman in the security camera footage you sent. What are the odds she turned up here and in your shelter too?"

"Pretty slim. I've no idea why he would be with her."

"Oh can't you?" Her voice turned grim. "What an innocent you are. You wouldn't believe the people that show up, 'just wanting to give a child a home.' Yeah, right."

"Yikes. Send me her photo, and I'll pass that information on to the authorities. Authority, who is currently my roommate. I repeat, I'm keeping Bam Bam—Balam—close by me. And if his father needs a sponsor or an attorney, put my name down. I'm not letting this family get thrown back into or across the Rio Grande."

She took a minute to curse, just on general principles. She sent the photo immediately afterwards. It had the person of interest circled, Candace Dagny. Connections started sparking in my brain. What a coincidence. Candace was the blonde woman who volunteered to care for Bam Bam the first night. She went to the immigration center and then tried to get to her home near Austin but couldn't make it because of the storm, and Bam Bam just happened to travel with her. Nope. Not buying it. She wasn't getting within twenty feet of the child now. I'd set Cupcake to guard him if I had to.

I put down the phone and bounced the boy in the air. "You hear that? Daddy is coming tomorrow to take you with him. You just keep telling people I'm your lawyer, and they have to talk to me. Got it?"

"Lah-or," he said. "Caw-bread?"

"Close enough. Let's go get some cornbread." I spun around a couple of times, making the boy giggle.

Out of the corner of my eye, I saw a flash of orange outside my office. I went to the doorway but didn't see anyone near. Still, it seemed like a good idea to shut the door.

"My friend Teresa says your name is Balam. Should I call you that?"

"Bam," he said, chewing on a finger. "Bam."

"Okay, we'll stick with Bam Bam for now. I'm not the kind of guy that has to anglicize other people's names, so you let me know when you want something more formal or accurate."

I danced down the gallery hall, singing ABBA's "Bang A Boomerang," a great nonsense song and great for bouncing toddlers. Johnny and Dianne joined in on their parts when I approached the kitchen. They greeted my news about Bam Bam's father with joy. They agreed to watch Bam Bam for a short time while I carried out my Cunning Plan, the idea provided earlier by Johnny. Forestalling separation anxiety, Dianne handed Bam Bam more sugar cookie bits.

Being a six-foot-three former basketball player, I had no problem nestling the turkey under my arm. I grabbed several plastic bags with the other hand before heading for the wood pile. I picked up Johnny's axe. After turning so that Bam Bam couldn't see me, I picked up Johnny's axe and brought the axe down hard on the breast bone. The turkey split in half. Now the parts would fit in the oven. I dealt it one more blow crosswise, just to make sure, and dumped the parts in the bags.

I carried them over my head in triumph, feeling like the huntsman who brought home a mammoth for dinner. We'd have one turkey, at least.

CHAPTER 5

WEDNESDAY NIGHT,
THANKSGIVING MINUS .5

Someone had set up a kiddie corral in the dining area near the kitchen so their parents could help get dinner ready. A riot of aromas hit my nose as Johnny combined multiple dishes from multiple cultures to stretch out our food supply. His menu style tends to be closer to collision than fusion, courtesy of his Jewish grandmother, Vietnamese grandfather, French mother, and college housemates that included Mexican American, Sri Lankan, Black, Italian, and other Asian cultures. We frequently ate tacos and samosas for dinner, if not spring rolls and spaghetti.

I deposited Bam Bam in the corral and inched away step by step, talking to him all the while. I made sure I could see him from anywhere in the kitchen. I wasn't going to lose him now, not when he was so close to rejoining his family.

A happy side effect of my axe work was that the turkey pieces also fit into the refrigerators. Not the same one, but I was still pleased. Just a few more hours, and they'd meet their destiny in the oven.

Candace Dagny marched to the edge of the kitchen while dragging two suitcases and a three-foot duffle bag, all on wheels. I looked up from shoving turkey legs on top of the already broken strawberry-rhubarb pie. No one would notice another dent or two. I caught sight of her orange scarf before her chalkboard-screechy voice demanded that I talk to her privately. I glanced toward Bam Bam, living up to his nickname by hitting blocks with other blocks. I didn't go any further than the center of the gallery, where we could still see each other.

Johnny and Dianne, nonchalant, wandered over at this hint of trouble. Johnny's eyes traveled from Candace to me and back again, calculating.

Candace snapped, "I can't find that lady who owns the house, so I'm telling you. This is the worst place I've ever stayed."

I countered, "We're a disaster shelter, not a B&B."

"You ought to be fired! The beds are uncomfortable, the food is horrible, animals are all over the place, no privacy at all, and people tramping all over the place at all hours of the night. That crazy lady in pink threatened to hit me with her stick, just because I was going to a different bathroom than the one nearest me. It was disgusting with all the little brats using it."

"I thought you loved children," I murmured.

She ignored me. "And then she had the nerve to walk with me to another one and wait for me! Well, I'm leaving right now. I heard the water's receding."

My glance toward Bam Bam took in the backyard too, where the water was not receding, just holding steady. Using an old trick for pretending to look in someone's eyes, I refocused my gaze not on her face, ugly with rage, but on the orange scarf around her neck.

Orange, just like the flash of orange I noticed from my office. I mentally kicked myself for not shutting the door, despite having a child in one arm, phone in the other. She'd heard my conversation with Teresa. I fiddled with my phone to send an SOS text to Officer Al.

"You don't want to be too hasty, Candace," I soothed. "You don't know if the roads are clear. It doesn't take much water to sweep a car away."

"That's just a myth. I'm not spending another minute here! You can't stop me."

I held up my hands. "I wouldn't try to. You're not a prisoner." In my mind, I added *Yet*. "I'm just concerned about your safety."

She sniffed and thrust her baggage in Johnny's direction. "You, take my bags to the car. The silver Lexus in the front lot."

Dianne's face tensed as her eyebrows snapped together. I could feel my face do the same thing. So the short Asian guy was the bellhop? I opened my mouth to deliver an anti-racist diatribe, but I didn't get a word out before Johnny bowed low from the waist.

"Yes, ma'am." He pushed down restaurant trash in the open duffle bag before he grabbed all the handles. "May I give you some spring rolls to take with you? I'm happy to include other dishes too. You don't know what condition your home will be in, and restaurants still aren't open.

She opened and shut her mouth, changing gears. "Yes. It's the least you could do."

"Happy to do so, ma'am. It will take only a minute."

Dianne inched toward me to say, as Candace followed Johnny to the kitchen. "Has he been watching old Charlie Chan movies?"

"I suspect Johnny has a Cunning Plan," I replied. I sent a longer text with more details to Officer Al.

"Ma'am, may I remove the trash from the duffle bag first?" Johnny called as he pulled on food-handling gloves—overkill, I thought. "It looks like the remains of a drive-through meal."

Candace had followed him close to the kitchen, where people still scurried around, preparing the next meal. Non-preparers gathered in expectation of setting the table. Not Candace—she wasn't going to start helping at this stage.

She waved a hand at Johnny. "Oh—certainly. I'd forgotten I stopped for something on the way here."

After he removed the chicken strips and their paper trash and tenderly substituted egg rolls, dinner rolls, and other nearby items, he wheeled the luggage toward the front door.

"Are you sure you wouldn't like to stay a few minutes more?" I asked her. "Dianne's tamales will be ready any minute, and they are worth any amount of waiting."

"Any minute now," Dianne chorused, with a gesture toward the oven.

Candace made a face like she'd been offered fried cow patties. "No, I think not. You, put everything in the trunk," she called after Johnny.

"Let us check your sleeping area and make sure you haven't left anything behind," I called after her in desperation.

She ignored me and barreled out the front door, stopping only to wave the key to unlock her car.

"Does she have something to do with Bam Bam? Is that why you tried to keep her here? " Dianne whispered as I dropped into a chair by the kiddie corral. I ruffled Bam Bam's hair and nodded.

A police siren whooped for a second. Dianne and I stared at each other for half a second. I scooped up Bam Bam and ran after her to the front porch.

Officer Al had pulled up behind the silver Lexus, blocking its exit. We couldn't hear what he was saying to Candace, but we could hear her just fine. He had no right to prevent her from leaving. She'd have his badge for sure. She demanded he get out of her way right now.

Officer Al raised his voice to shut her up. "Ma'am, there's been a complaint. I need you to come down to the station and answer some questions.

"Complaint? Who made a complaint about me? The nerve!" She could shout louder.

"The Fort Walter children's holding center wants your input on a missing child. Ma'am, it's best to conduct this interview at the station."

"That filthy place! I went there to adopt a poor immigrant child in need."

"Children there have not been released for adoption. Most will be reunited with their families."

"It was the most horrible place. I couldn't abandon the poor boy in those conditions. I have a compassionate heart. No one stopped me, so I thought everything was fine."

Everything was fine because she hid him in a duffle bag and brought him here, still hidden. She didn't dare let us connect the two of them. My blood boiled. I held him closer.

While she continued to harangue Officer Al, Johnny edged away from the scene and returned to the house in a fast walk.

"Don't let them leave," he whispered to us and kept moving toward the house.

Dianne and I shrugged at each other and descended the seven steps into the front yard. Candace waved her arms and scuttled this way and that, the better to keep them out of Officer Al's cuffs.

The ground was still squishy, close to liquid. The air smelled like moldy everything. Intermittent plops of rain dropped from a sky reluctant to give up its tantrum. We were halfway to the car when Bam Bam stiffened and screamed. Surprised, I almost dropped him as he squirmed and thrashed. Everyone turned and stared. Officer Al took advantage of the distraction to cuff Candace, which set her screaming even louder.

"Ma'am, you have to come to the station," he insisted.

"Bam Bam—Balam Caal—always got upset whenever she was nearby," I declared in my courtroom voice. I muttered to Dianne, "Stay here and stall them." I ran back to the house with the sobbing boy. On the porch, I passed Johnny on his way back out, carrying a mostly empty trash bag. I ignored him. I had a child to comfort.

The aroma of popcorn and forlorn boredom hit me when I opened the front door. The kids and adults watching TV in the gallery didn't even glance at us, despite Bam Bam's howls. Brightly colored muppets danced on the screen. I'm glad I grew up in the age of smaller TVs. I would have been terrified of giant weird creatures on screens taller than me.

I headed for my office. I settled in one of my client chairs and rocked back and forth as much as I could in a non-rocking chair. I assured him that I'd never let the horrible woman near him again, words he couldn't understand. So I sang "I Have a Dream" even softer and slower than ABBA intended.

He'd settled into low moans when Johnny and Dianne returned. They joined the song, Dianne taking over the melody just before the high part and Johnny and I in harmony.

"You know I heard back from Teresa at Los Anfitriones," I told them. "She confirmed that a child is missing from the center. Even more significant is that Candace Dagny visited both the center and our shelter. She probably smuggled him out of there and into here in her big duffle bag."

Johnny nodded, having worked out the duffle bag's role.

"Just walked in and took a kid?" asked Dianne, skeptical.

I continued, "Monday was so chaotic that it was easy not to be noticed in either place. Here, she sent him into the kid room and later came back to register herself. That evening she offered to take care of him, probably to give herself some credibility when it came time to settle him permanently. It made her furious when we didn't allow that. I think she overheard me talking to Teresa this afternoon and decided to scram. She knew it was in her best interest to be elsewhere."

Johnny explained his part. "I asked her if I could clean out the trash from her duffle before I put more food in it, and she said yes. I used gloves and a clean trash bag. I hope that exchange counts as her offering me her DNA. Hers should be on the wrappers, and the child's DNA should be on the half-chewed chicken sticks. I gave the bag to Officer Al for evidence."

I couldn't help grinning. "He should be able to work with that. Hey, kid, what say we veg out to another episode of *Fraggle Rock*?"

Bam Bam ran out of tears and reached for the fidget toys on my desk. He didn't object to my plan.

Everyone laughed more that evening than they had for days, even with the kids and dogs wilder than ever. The Very Good Kitties escaped the clinic again and zoomed all over the house. Somehow all the shenanigans were funny now with the holiday approaching and the skies cleared.

Cupcake too reached the end of her ability to behave. Escaping from her crate when Darryl tried to give her more water, she romped up and down the halls, deaf to suggestions from her officer when he returned. Even past lights out, giggles rose from the cots wherever she went.

I suggested swapping security rounds with Officer Al so he could corral his dog and I could finish my turkey prep. Worn out, Cupcake flopped in her crate, panting and grinning. Officer Al put his pillow in the crate doorway so she could cuddle next to him.

Once again, I rocked Bam Bam to sleep while I tiptoed through my security rounds. But instead of taking him upstairs to bed, I made a pallet inside the kiddie corral by the kitchen and laid him there, always in my sight.

With the house now shrouded in dark silence, the quiet after the storm felt strange. The wind still whistled around corners, but it sounded more like a flute than a tornado. I rejoiced that the weather had given up trying to kill us for half a minute.

In the kitchen, I heard other noises from the walk-in pantry. Only one person makes angry, choked-off sobs like that.

Dianne slumped on the floor, legs stretched out in front of her. Her feet stuck out, even beyond the open folded doors, because we always shove in bulk boxes until Johnny or Chantal complains about not being able to reach the back shelf. A long oblong pan sat beside her. She bowed her head in deep mourning. The closer I got, the more corn and spicy pork aromas wafted my way.

"Dianne? Everything okay?"

She raised her head and spit words at me. "Everything is not okay. That beast Cupcake ran through the kitchen when I was taking the tamales out of the oven. She knocked the pan out of my hands and now they're ruined. And my hand's burned."

I retrieved burn salve from the first aid kit. Johnny keeps one in every room. "They fell on the floor? We could wash them off and not tell anybody."

She accepted the burn salve, but her glare could have stripped paint. "No! They're broken to bits, and I don't have time to do another batch, even if I had the ingredients."

I moved the tamales tray to sit beside her, but it looked like the cats had knocked off half the items from the shelves. I put back a few cans and packages and discovered a big box underneath that took up the rest of the pantry floor space. I leaned against the island in the middle of the kitchen instead.

"Drawing on my expert knowledge of Guadalupe Dianne Cortez, I postulate that something's wrong besides scrambled tamales and scramble-brained huskies. Normal response for this woman would be to yeet the broken food into the sun and maybe the husky too, if she came within reach. Come on, Dianne. I've thought something was wrong from the moment you staggered in from the rain on Monday."

"Madre de Dios, JD, my holiday dinner with my family is ruined."

"I submit testimony that Ms. Cortez used to calculate how little time she could spend at home for the holidays without making her family mad."

"Shut up, JD." She sighed so long it could have been a vocal exercise. "My grandmother. Abuela. She's sick. They don't think she'll last long, and the whole family was supposed to come for Thanksgiving dinner. And I'm here, stuck in a stupid flood, only proving my mother's point that I shouldn't have moved so far away."

"Yeah, video calls just aren't the same."

"I can't even do that," Dianne blurted. "My family decided to put my MultiABBA cardboard cutout on the opposite side of the room from Abuela. She doesn't see very well."

I couldn't help laughing, which made Dianne glare harder. I gasped, "It might work, if she buys that you'd show up to a family gathering wearing a yellow bandage dress."

"My sisters are going to hang their clothes over Cardboard Me." After a moment, Dianne couldn't help laughing too.

"Pics or it didn't happen," I said.

"They better take photos!"

"If Bam Bam's father can get here tomorrow, the waters must be receding. I bet you can be on the road no later than Friday, maybe our guests too." I tried to sit beside her again, making another attempt to push the box out of the way.

"JD, not everybody's going to leave immediately. They might not have a home to go to, or it might be too damaged to live in."

"My one hope is the restaurants and grocery stores will be open again, or we're going to be serving air with a side of sunlight." I returned a few cans to the shelves and shoved the box again. It didn't want to move, but I kept trying. "What is in this box anyway? What do we have that takes up this much room?"

Dianne helped me push it into the light. I pulled open the flaps. The box was full of cans and packaged food. A note on letter-sized paper lay on top. I picked it up.

Mrs. Ly, Johnny's grandmother, had written it late Monday night. We hadn't seen her since, because Officer Al took her to the other shelters in town.

Under the exact date and time, leaving no doubt from whom Johnny inherited his precision, she wrote, "This box contains food that people donated when they entered the shelter. There's also a ham and some pies that I put in the porch refrigerator by the grill. I'm too tired to find anyone to tell tonight."

"I bet that's what she was yelling at us on her way out. Look, JD! Real cranberry sauce, the kind everyone likes! And more cornbread and stuffing mixes for your turkey."

"Alongside my turkey," I corrected. I got to my feet and opened the second refrigerator. I pulled out the turkey parts and put them on the island. "After I roast this dismembered bird for eternity, I'll set the pieces over your ruined tamales, and we'll have tamale-stuffed turkey."

Dianne's face blossomed into a real smile for the first time in days. "That will make the brown population of the shelter very happy."

"And maybe with enough cornbread dressing on the side, the rest won't be too unhappy. I see a couple more boxes of stuffing."

I grew more cheerful as we sorted through the food, enough for several days more of meals, especially with the promise of more from the porch refrigerator. "Do you remember the story of the loaves and fishes? Jesus had this big crowd to feed, and the only food they had was a little bit of bread and a few fishes that some kid brought."

"The nuns would revoke my high school diploma if I didn't."

"I think it went down like this. Some kid steps up and hands over his Lunchable and Jesus blesses it like it's Sunday brunch. And the adults who were going to sneak off and eat the meals they brought for themselves got embarrassed and handed over everything they had, and magically there was enough for all. Everyone said, whoa, Jesus did a miracle, when really it was just everybody doing what they could, like here, when I didn't know what to feed Bam Bam, but the lady from Guatemala did. And another lady gave him some clothes, and Cupcake barked and alerted us when Candace would have snuck in your room and stolen him in the night. Come to think of it, she must have been hiding in the closet, behind the cardboard MultiABBAs. The lights were out, thanks to her, and I couldn't see all the way inside."

Dianne sniffed. "You don't think that's a miracle? Everybody working together and sharing what they have?"

I thought about it and put an arm around her shoulder. "You might be right. Is that the cue for a song of thanksgiving?"

Apparently it was. We settled on "Thank You for the Music" and sang it all the way through (adjusting lyrics as they occurred to us) while we finished our preparations for the next day. I sang it to Bam Bam too when I hauled him upstairs to bed one last time. Maybe he'd remember his recent traumas the rest of his life, but I hoped he'd remember the intervening angels too.

EPILOGUE
THANKSGIVING

Candace Dagny was arrested for kidnapping. She spent her Thanksgiving in jail. I'm guessing that she wasn't thankful. Officer Al brought Mrs. Ly back to Gregg House for Thanksgiving dinner, which was, in my humble opinion, fabulous, particularly the tamale-stuffed turkey with cornbread dressing on the side. I assembled the cooked turkey parts over the broken tamales in an abstract representation, Johnny having dissuaded me from using duct tape.

Bam Bam's father, Adelmo Caal, arrived with Teresa in time to share the meal. That was Dianne's cue that the roads had opened. She was on the road to Garland before the newcomers were seated with full plates in front of them.

Full plates, even with caw-bread, couldn't distract the boy and his father from each other. I couldn't understand a word they said, but I know joy when I see it. I'd never seen Bam Bam smile and laugh before. Though it was a happy sight, I blinked my eyes rapidly when they left shortly afterwards.

The last thing I saw and heard was Balam twisting in his father's arms and reaching out to me as he called, "Lah-or."

PART TWO
CHRISTMAS PARADE

CHAPTER 1
THURSDAY NIGHT

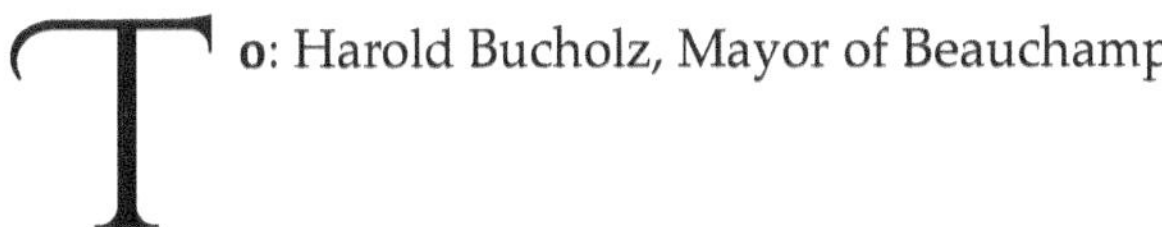

To: Harold Bucholz, Mayor of Beauchamp

From: JD Thompson, Attorney at Law

Issue: Beauchamp's first Guadalupe Day-Christmas parade and adjacent events

P R I V A T E

For Your Eyes Only

Dear Mayor Bucholz,

I received your request for a description of last Saturday's first ever Guadalupe/Christmas parade and the adjacent events.

Look, Harry, I was there, but there's no way I was an impartial observer. All I can tell you is what I saw, heard, and felt. I don't claim it's the truth or the only truth.

You're probably familiar with the origin of the parade. Father Emilio of the Catholic Church had long wanted to hold a celebration for Our Lady of Guadalupe on or near her feast day of December 12. The Beauchamp Chamber of Commerce dreamed of a Christmas parade, and the two groups formed an uneasy alliance to combine resources, with the church objecting to Santa, reindeer, and snowmen, and the Chamber thinking the religious part boring. The church did provide flower-laden floats featuring every person in town named Guadalupe. Those included some beautiful young Latinas, but the Guadalupes ranged in age from nine months to seventy-eight and one fifty-eight-year-old man, lacking in the correct amount of eye candy, according to some.

Unbeknownst to the church and the Chamber, other forces were at work.

I entered the picture the Thursday before, when the Promise of a New Day club held their monthly meeting at Gregg House.

When Mrs. Ly turned Gregg House over to her grandson, veterinarian Dr. John Ky Ly (tenor), and his college housemates and fellow band members of MultiABBA—me as attorney (bass-baritone), accountants Dianne Cortez (alto) and Chantal Gaumont (soprano)—she expected us to continue her charitable works. Later this month, we'll host her traditional open house and holiday party. You are, of course, invited as is the rest of Beauchamp and its environs. MultiABBA will naturally provide the music, a mixture of ABBA songs and holiday music. All the holidays.

Black Orchid Enterprises, our umbrella organization, continues to furnish meeting space for the various nonprofits that Mrs. Ly supports —Boy Scouts, Beauchamp Library Board, Alvarez County Young Mothers, Friends of Animals, and the town do-gooders, Promise of a New Day. One of the Black Orchids always looks in on the meetings so we can say we know what's going on in the house. Thursday was my turn.

Twelve women, looking like the United Nations in their various skin colors and outfits, gathered in our living room. Our house cats wove around their ankles, sometimes jumping on a lap. That always stopped the meeting so everyone could coo over the darling kitty.

Doria Langston, who succeeded Mrs. Ly as president, said after the usual meeting-opening rituals, "JD, we're glad you're here tonight. We need your advice."

You'll remember Mrs. Langston, a native Beauchamp Black woman who recently retired from the City Clerk's office. She fiercely championed anyone who needed help, but anyone trying to put one over on her or the city lived to regret it. She was also one of the Beauchamp's DC Five, and if you've forgotten that caper, all I can say is that I and half of Washington, DC, have not. She used to wear the drab plumage worthy of a career admin assistant, but she's cast off that look since her retirement. That night her garb came straight out of Africa—a long, flared dress with voluminous sleeves made up in a bright waxy fabric of bold, splashy patterns and an elaborate turban to match. She looked like the leader she was, with no longer any need to hide it.

On this occasion the group was all women, mostly over sixty, that dangerous age when they no longer give a good door slam what anybody thinks. They've put up with the world's nonsense as long as they're going to, and they are now making changes.

Half of them dressed like Miss Doria, rejecting their professional drag for whatever pleased them. In addition to African garb, I saw Mexican blouses and gathered skirts in fierce colors, an Asian haori, and an Indian subcontinent salwar kameez. The woman in jeans and a tie-dyed T-shirt looked staid by comparison. Other women dressed like they had always dressed, fortunately not in miniskirts and go-go boots, but tailored shirts and slacks, usually in subdued colors.

And then there was Marjorie Feral. (Because my Southern mother raised me right, I refer to all women over fifty by their last names and honorific unless I know them better, when using "Miss" and their first name is allowed. Marjorie refused that courtesy, saying "Call me Marjorie. Not Marge.") She has a deep, obvious bond with her inner child, who's around ten. She likes pink. She likes all the brands designed to appeal to young girls—Hello Kitty, Barbie, Rainbow Brite, Strawberry Shortcake, and the like. Today she wore a Lisa Frank shirt, full of big-eyed cutified animals in a revised rainbow scheme of pink, coral, yellow, spring green, turquoise, and amethyst. She would have looked exactly like my twin sisters at age ten, but for her Texas-fried skin, long wild white hair, and her cane, also in Lisa Frank colors.

My eyes naturally went to Marjorie and her clothes of many colors, but I forced my gaze back to Miss Doria and the evening's agenda.

To my surprise, the meeting wasn't about paying off school lunch debt, providing low-income medical services, establishing community gardens, serving meals to school children during summer and holidays, or any other community cause. They had gathered to take care of one of their own.

"JD, you remember Lily Jensen?" Miss Doria nodded toward a tiny White woman with wispy white hair, one of the subdued dressers. "She's your neighbor across the street." She waved her hand in the general direction of outdoors.

I exchanged smiles with Miss Lily. I'd have described her house as cattywampus across the street, Beauchamp Park being directly across from us, but it was true that I could see her collapsing frame house from our front porch.

Most of the houses in Beauchamp were built long ago, starting with Gregg House in 1897, and then jumping to mid-twentieth century. Their conditions range from insufficient walls and roofs to spiffed up for a Southern Living photoshoot. Miss Lily's was closer to the lower end, but it had enough structure to keep out the elements. She and her husband had moved into Beauchamp proper after selling their farm seven years ago, and entropy had taken over since his death some two years ago.

"Lily's moving, for all I tell her that nobody can force her out and she should just ignore that…witch." Miss Doria took a deep breath to swallow the words she really wanted to use. She addressed my bewildered expression. "Mindy Clement, the deputy's wife. The one trying to get everyone within five blocks of downtown to establish a homeowners' association so she can drive out anyone who doesn't maintain their house to her standards."

"Neighborhood for the 1%?" muttered Marjorie.

Acknowledging Marjorie with a slight nod, Miss Doria continued,

"Hasn't she called on you?" She scratched the chin of our brown tabby cat.

"Well, not me personally." I called across to the hall to my partner Dianne Cortez in her office, one of the turrets facing the road. "Dianne, have you heard from a woman trying to establish an HOA?"

With her own cat, a flame point Siamese, in her arms, Dianne came to the doorway and leaned against it, followed by her friend and bandmate Chantal Gaumont. "Yes. I told her—" Dianne cut loose with a torrent of Spanish invective that I shouldn't translate. "She asked if I'd been here long enough to understand American. I told her 'Yes,' and then 'No,' both complete sentences. I didn't take the documents she waved at me, and I haven't seen her since."

"We can't be having that nonsense," Chantal declared. She pushed past Dianne and pulled another chair into a circle. "Are you guys going to do something about her? I can tell you what my aunties did."

I eyed Chantal, whose deep brown eyes gleamed. "Keep it legal, Chantal."

"Well, that's boring."

"We can be legal and effective," I declared. "If anyone has a copy of Mindy's docs, I'd like to look them over. If she's harassing people into selling their homes—that's just wrong."

"I'll get my copy for you tomorrow," said Lily. "It's too late for me, but maybe you can help someone else. I'm ready to sell. My son in Chicago has a spare bedroom for me." Her shoulders slumped.

Mrs. Langston objected, "Honey, you don't want to go to Chicago. It's cold there."

Lily gave her friends a cheerless smile. "It's going to be cold here if I can't get the house and my heating system repaired."

"Let Dianne and me look into getting you a grant," I urged. "There are organizations that help people get their homes in shape."

Miss Lily shook her head. "And what happens in a few years when I need more repairs? And who's going to pay my electric bill, especially when we have colder or warmer temperatures than usual, which seems to be every year now. I'm tired of trying to keep my house and yard in shape." Her lower lip trembled and her voice wobbled. "I told myself at least I'd find my engagement and wedding band if I sorted all my possessions. I kept taking them off to sew or clean house, and I haven't been able to find them for months.

"There's still time," Miss Doria said in comforting tones. "Even if Lily is determined to leave, these grants sound like something we should know about to help other people."

"I can't say I want to go to Chicago, but I do want to get rid of all the extra stuff in the house. My children don't want it. So many things we kept from the farm, like we were ever going to need a tractor again. So many things from the kids, things they don't care about anymore. I have photos. I have videos. I don't need the physical objects—well, except my rings." Her voice still shook. "And I have so many supplies for my sewing and crafts! Two bedrooms full, and they're encroaching into my bedroom too."

"You're not getting rid of all that, are you?" asked Miss Doria. To me, she explained, "Lily is the best seamstress. She made her kids' clothes and costumes for every town event, whether her kids were part of it or not. For the Guadalupe Parade this Saturday, she made most of the capes."

"Christmas Parade," said Marjorie, sotto voce. Half of the room nodded along.

Miss Doria insisted, "The capes are for the Guadalupe celebration." The other half of the room nodded. "Lily made them from blue satin with a star pattern and gold ruffles over the head and around the edges, so they'd look like Our Lady of Guadalupe with her full-body halo. Really clever."

The Latina contingent murmured in approval.

Miss Doria sighed. "We don't want you to leave, Lily. But if you're determined, we'll help you."

Miss Lily swallowed back tears. "You people talked me into charging for my work, but sewing just doesn't pay much. I'll have only one bedroom in Chicago. Where am I going to put an embroidery machine, a serger, a long arm quilter, or even just a plain sewing machine, much less a lifetime collection of fabric and craft notions? I'm going to sell it all."

All the ladies, including Chantal, sat up straighter.

"Embroidery machine?" she asked.

"Long arm?" asked Miss Doria.

Her grandson Darryl Swann, our intern, tiptoed in from the kitchen. "Glitter? Crystals?"

"So much glitter, so many crystals," confirmed Miss Lily. "And spangles and fabric paint and boxes of things I've forgotten about."

"Obviously, you have things people want. How are you advertising?" I asked. I'd seen a Yard Sale poster made of dollar-store cardboard and markers on a stake near the ground in front of her house.

Miss Lily's voice swelled with pride. "Oh, I've done a lot! Last weekend I announced my sale in Sunday School. I put a sign out by the road. Everybody travels on Louisiana Street. I was going to put an ad in the newspaper, but I missed the deadline, and it's published only weekly. And I tacked an index card on the community boards at the Senior Center and Casa Gracias."

I glanced at Darryl, who tried not to roll his eyes. They watered with the effort of holding them wide open. He too was taught to respect his elders.

I waited several beats until it was clear Miss Lily had reached the end of her efforts. "What about social media? I'm sure there are local online groups who'd be interested."

Miss Lily raised her hands, as though to ward off evil. "Oh, I don't know how to do that. Does anybody really look at it?"

I drew a breath and counted to ten to keep my face straight. "Sometimes. You can never have too much publicity. Or so my social media guru tells me. Darryl?"

He saluted in a manner unknown to any military organization. "On it, boss! Am I getting paid?"

"Yes, you're on the clock."

"Alrighty then! Granny, I need the names of your quilt groups. I bet they've all got online presence. And I know so many people interested in…um…costuming and crafts." Darryl, deep in his element, danced his fingers across his phone.

"Really, Darryl? How is that?" asked his grandmother.

Crashing back to earth, Darryl twitched. He opened his mouth and shut it.

I answered for him. "Darryl's been doing work with his college drama department. And he helps us with the band, like costumes, production, and the like." I didn't know if he wanted me to mention his singing.

He flashed me a grateful smile and sighed. "Yeah. Like that. I better get to work."

His reception desk and laptop weren't that far away from the group, so the rest of the meeting was punctuated with his requests for more fabric, craft, and farm groups to target. Because the ladies wanted to get started on the grant work, I sent Chantal to fetch Dianne. She does the money work, being our chief accountant.

With that last delegation, I thought I was free.

CHAPTER 2

SATURDAY MORNING

Darryl brought me the HOA paperwork after he finished taking photos of Lily's treasures on Friday afternoon, and I skimmed it before I declared the workweek over.

I planned to talk to Miss Lily on Monday, but Chantal had other ideas. On Saturday morning she rousted me out of bed at What The—o'clock so I could help her haul over our contribution to the sale. That included every gourd and pumpkin still on the vine in our garden. We'd let them grow to see how long the weather would hold off killing them. To give you an idea about December in Texas, I was wearing Birks, cargo shorts, and a band T-shirt inside out and backwards—not on purpose. I just wasn't fully awake when I got dressed. Chantal wore a tropical-patterned halter top over jorts, socks with her sandals, and a sweater tied around her waist. As a New Orleans native, she feels the cold more than most of us.

We arrived an hour before the sale, but the yard was already full. Darryl waited until Friday night to send out his posts in hopes of controlling the early birds, but to no avail.

Marjorie Feral had pulled her trailer into Miss Lily's driveway. I blinked at her bright glory—a Hello Kitty tunic over Barbie-pink bike shorts and sneakers. She was slapping on pricing stickers with a tagging gun.

"Isn't this great?" she bellowed. She'd honed her supersized outdoor voice while teaching classes in the park. She shows senior citizens how to use their canes as singlesticks in a Regency style of fencing. "I was going to take this stuff to Goodwill, but better if it can bring in a few bucks for Lily. I brought my friends from Austin's Austenites too. We're always looking for good deals on fabric and notions."

She made a vague gesture toward a huddled group of mature women, but I had no trouble identifying the Regency reenactors. They wore bonnets and long, gauzy, high-waisted gowns.

Marjorie yanked a dining room chair out of the trailer. "Any excuse to dress up, you know? Also, it's a good way to match colors. Most of us are adding to our outfits rather than starting from scratch. I didn't want to tear up mine with all the hauling and arranging, so I brought samples instead." She waved a large index card with fabric squares glued to it. Her eyes narrowed and fastened on her prey, a length of royal blue wool in Miss Lily's arms. "That would make a good Spencer jacket. You keep emptying the trailer while I check it out, okay?"

She sprinted to the front door where Miss Lily stood clutching several bolts of fabric to her chest. Her eyes darted around the swelling crowd in panic.

Chantal yanked my arm. "You can do that right after you finish with our stuff. Just artistically arrange the pumpkins under that big tree by the road. They'll attract attention, not that we need it. I'm going to help Lily. She's floundering. I wasn't planning on running a yard sale today, but here we are."

She was qualified. Chantal always ran our move-out sales in college. As I stacked the pumpkins under the tree, maybe not artistically, I saw relief flood Miss Lily's face when Chantal took the fabric bolts and Marjorie's pricing gun.

"Excuse me, can you move those pumpkins back further from the sidewalk? I wouldn't want somebody to kick them during our routines."

The voice was high for a man, low for a woman, rich in timbre. I looked up to see someone my size in full makeup, clad in ruffles and bows, twirling a frilly umbrella in white-gloved hands. I blinked, confused only a moment as to gender, but very confused at a drag queen's presence at a Saturday morning yard sale.

Drag queens. A dozen or so. Before you get any strange ideas, they looked more like Rebecca of Sunnybrook Farm than Dolly Parton. Giant, economy-sized Rebeccas, but all perfect ladies in high-necked, long-sleeved, old-fashioned cotton dresses with many petticoats.

"We're the Parasol Protectors. I'm Luscious Laveau, drill captain. We show up whenever the family needs protecting, like story hour at the library. So many people wanted to come to the boondocks for this sale, and you never know who you're going to find in the wilds of Texas. Also, we wanted to practice our new dance routine."

"Glad to have you. I hope you have nothing to do besides dance." My heart warmed, talking to a kindred soul. I must have gone to classes sometimes in college, because I have a diploma, but a lot of my memories involve walking people to and from the library at night and rescuing my housemates from creepy dates.

Luscious called out to our intern Darryl as he guided his grandmother across the street, "Hey, Darryl, we gonna see Swannie Chalant today?"

Darryl held his grandmother's arm with one hand as she took a careful step up onto the curb. In his other hand he held a lawn and leaf bag, stuffed tight. He jumped when Luscious called to him. He almost knocked Miss Doria over, or so she said. He dropped the bag and used both hands to steady his grandmother, who then scolded him as a toaster and a mini blender rolled out of the bag.

"Sorry, Gran." He swallowed and stooped down to reclaim the runaway merchandise before answering Luscious. "Probably not. Swannie had other commitments this morning."

"Well, you tell her we're happy to see her whenever she can make it," The drill captain swished her parasol in a figure eight.

"Will do," he promised.

Miss Doria commanded, "Darryl, hustle yourself and get things set out to sell. People are already here."

Darryl hustled.

"Toodle-oo," called Luscious after him.

I didn't understand all the layers of their conversation, but the parasol distracted me. Its lacy, ruffled panels gathered around an end tip (with yet another ruffle, for a rose-like appearance). But the tip was longer than normal, resembling a stiletto knife. Very like a stiletto, though I wasn't going to check.

Groups of people poured in, thanks to Darryl's usual brilliant social media work. Some buyers, like the quilters, cosplayers, reenactors, and theatre costumers, headed to the mounds of sewing supplies.

The farm women seemed split between buyers and sellers. Two women in plaid cotton shirts rode in on a tractor towing a full trailer of donations. Another woman driving a tractor with a full trailer parked on the side street. Other outdoorsy women headed for Miss Lily's tractor and farm tools. Two rode in on their horses, mostly for the outing, it seemed, because they stayed mounted and chatted with those on the ground. I wondered why all the farmers seemed to be women until I heard one of them refer to their group as Sappho in the Fields. I'd heard lesbians buying farms was the latest trend, but I didn't know they'd come to Beauchamp.

Children squirmed though the crush of shoppers with no apparent direction or purpose. None of the people old enough to be their parents paid them any mind.

In addition to their G-rated dance routines, suitable for any middle school drill team, the Protectors also acted as guides, sending newcomers to the right place to either deposit wares or buy them. They themselves took turns darting into the sale. Chantal, Darryl, Marjorie, Miss Leigh, Miss Doria, and other Promisers did their best to establish order. They enlisted a church pastor to auction the big-ticket items and set up an auction schedule. They wrangled cash boxes. Pricing stickers and signs popped up on the display tables. Chantal barked orders through a bullhorn. The event reminded me of spring break on Padre Island or Big Game Day at college, except people weren't as drunk. Yet.

Many sewing supply customers had kids in tow. The kids ran by, punching and tripping each other. Every time I turned around, they zoomed past again.

At a conservative estimate, half of the county had converged on Miss Lily's yard. The other half were headed for the morning's parade several blocks away, but those walking by stopped for just a quick peek or to join in the dance routine of Parasol Protectors.

At one point, the dance line went down the entire length of Miss Lily's sidewalk, two lots' worth, with Protectors and volunteers from ages in the single digits to almost triple, the eldest ones dancing around their canes or walkers.

A good time was had by all, except a couple of dudes on the opposite side of the street. They might have called their rural diner garb rugged, but it looked ragged to me. They glared at the chorus line as they marched back and forth, angrier on each pass. They pointed with stabbing fingers at Luscious Laveau and the troupe, who waved at them. The guys turned brick red.

Finally they moved on. Maybe they didn't want to be late to the parade. I took comfort in knowing that Gregg House's security cameras, necessary for Johnny's veterinary drugs, would have captured them.

Beauchamp restauranteurs spontaneously appeared with carts and food, so far without alcohol. I bought a couple of kolaches from Mary Chang of the Golden Donut and shoved my way across the lawn to Miss Lily, still on her front steps, still worried. She accepted a kolache but just clutched it in one hand while she surveyed the chaos.

Catching sight of a new arrival at the curb, I said, "Would you like me to ask Officer Al to act as security? He must be off duty since he's escorting his aunt."

"That's a good idea," Miss Lily replied without looking at me. Her eyes darted around, never resting on anything or anyone. "I never found my rings. Now I'm scared they might be in one of these boxes. Darryl was so kind as to put everything out, but I'd hoped to go through it all one more time."

I sympathized, "I can't do anything about the ones that are already gone, but I can look through the remaining ones, if you like."

Finally, her pale blue eyes rested on my face. "Would you, JD? I'd feel so much better. Though I don't see how I could have missed them when I was sorting. But where could they be? I know they're just things, but still." Her lips trembled as she forced a smile.

"They're important things. I'll see what I can do, right after I talk to Officer Al."

On the upside, Officer Al was glad to act as security. He'd earn some money, and he wouldn't have to follow his aunt around the yard. Not as much, anyway. The first thing he did was order the kids out of the big tree by the road. Its branches were a perfect height for climbing. Also perfect for falling out of and breaking collar bones. I winced in memory.

On the downside, he'd brought his dog Cupcake, a blue-eyed, manic-looking, silver husky. Cupcake has a lot of training in police work, which she remembers when it suits her. Otherwise, she runs here, there, and everywhere. Other people had brought their dogs too —or maybe they were strays—but they recognized in Cupcake the leader they longed for. Cupcake did not disappoint, leading a boxer, Golden Lab, Dalmatian, German Shepherd, and many Heinz 57 varieties around and through the yard and to the food carts that might have treats for good dogs. Somehow the ever-growing string of kids always went in the opposite direction from the dogs.

When I saw Johnny pulling a wagon full of donations from our neighbor to the south, I helped him unload and asked him to fill in as a medic. Yes, he's a vet, but he's had first aid training. He could do minor patchwork and triage. Someone was bound to get hurt with all the energy and random motion in the area.

CHAPTER 3
YARD SALE EXTRAORDINAIRE

I know you want to know about the parade, Harry. But you've got to understand the background first.

After I arranged for a medic and security, I started searching for rings. I picked up a box of shiny charms to sort through. A woman smacked me in the mouth with a Laurel Burch handbag.

Chantal came to my rescue. "Don't worry, he's just… What are you doing, JD?"

"Looking for Miss Lily's rings." I licked the blood off my teeth and ran my hands through the kitschy doodads. Real jewelry would have been obvious. I handed the box to the shopper, a solid woman in the don't-ask-don't-tell age range with big Texas hair. "Here. It's yours. Right after you pay Chantal."

She snatched it out of my hands. "They're perfect for homecoming mums. I'll give you a dollar for them and these rolls of ribbon."

She held up a box of eight colors of industrial-sized ribbon rolls, the satin kind that people pinch, twist, braid, and loop into the monstrosities teenagers wear around their necks for homecoming.

Chantal sniffed. "You'll give me the marked price. It's too early in the day for deals. Besides, you busted my friend in the chops."

After completing the transaction, Chantal took charge of my project and handed me a roll of green stickers to put on each container that I searched. She asked the other cashiers to quickly search through any item that might conceal rings if the container didn't sport a green sticker.

"What is going on here?" a woman shrieked. "Do you have a permit for this event? I live on the next block, and you're making an ungodly racket."

"I don't know, but we've got a lawyer," Chantal replied. "You go talk to him. Who are you, anyway?"

"This is Mindy Clement," said Miss Lily as loudly as she could.

"*Mindy*? This is Mindy?" demanded Chantal. "Our lawyer really wants to talk to you about your HOA. Everybody, this is *Mindy*. You've heard of her. Mindy, lots of people want to talk to you."

A crowd swelled around Mindy. Her eyes grew wide, and she stepped backwards, a mistake since she stumbled over a low table. Someone helped her up. I was glad to see the crowd didn't intend to tear her limb from limb. She scurried off, not having the same level of confidence.

I moved over to the clothing section. Pockets would be a great place to put rings and forget where they were. Also, I could search pockets faster than boxes.

I started with the tables of folded clothing because two women, both in country shirts and jeans, were looking through the rack of formals and hanger-worthy clothes. A wedding dress held their attention.

The one with short dark curls and an olive complexion said, "Anna, you wanted a wedding dress. If you like this one and it fits, let's get it. This one's bound to be cheaper than anything from a store."

Anna, taller with her silky strawberry blonde hair pulled back into a ponytail, coppery freckles dancing across her nose, shook her head. Her pale skin was closer to white than most people who claim that race, but somehow, she gave the impression of being bruised. "I *wanted* a big wedding, Ellen. But we're going to the courthouse. This dress is too fancy."

"We're getting *married* at the courthouse, Anna. You can wear whatever you want." Ellen took a deep breath, and said, like she was making a supreme sacrifice. "I'll even wear a dress, if you want me to."

A reluctant giggle emerged from Anna. "That would be almost worth it."

"Let's do it!" Ellen clapped her hands. "I'll send photos to my mother. She'll have to double her meds for the day. And we'll send photos to your parents' hometown newspaper. It'll serve them right, when they have to put up with congrats from all their churchy friends."

Anna hung on to a nearby chair as she collapsed into helpless laughter. By this time, Miss Lily had made her way down the porch steps and said they were welcome to come inside and try on the dress. Yes, she had made it for her daughter, now divorced.

Anna and Ellen told her how they'd bought a farm last year on the outskirts of Beauchamp near Miss Lily's old place, as it turned out. They'd planned a Thanksgiving wedding in Anna's hometown, until Anna's mother said she'd prayed about it and decided she couldn't attend such an abomination as her daughter's wedding to another woman. No, Anna couldn't talk to her father. He agreed with her mother, and Anna was no longer welcome in their home. Ellen's mother didn't want to hear from her until she was dating a man.

"It'll be a cold day in Texas when that happens," declared Ellen. "We never planned to invite her. We always knew Anna's family wasn't happy about us, but we never expected them to cut us out of their lives." She put an arm around Anna, whose head and shoulders sagged as she tried not to cry.

"You'll have a perfectly lovely wedding without them," said Miss Lily.

"But where?" sobbed Anna. "We were going to get married in my friend's gay-friendly church back home in St. Louis, but what's the point if my friends can't get there and my family won't come? I don't even want to ask the churches around here. I've seen their signs."

Miss Lily patted her arm. "You might be surprised. You'll find a place. If I'm still in this house, you can have it in my backyard. Now, let's find something for Ellen to wear."

"I said I'd wear a dress, and I will," declared Ellen as she pulled a simple purple scoop-necked formal from the rack. "This isn't half bad, for a dress. No frilly girly stuff anywhere."

"I made that for my granddaughter's prom. It's designed to show off the fabric," said Miss Lily, pointing out the rich silk.

"I want you to be comfortable, Ellen," objected Anna. She pushed clothes aside until she discovered a deep blue-green pantsuit fit for a presidential candidate.

I moved on to shaking out handbags while they tried on their outfits. All I had to do was hold up a purse and someone would snatch it. I didn't mind because I heard Darryl further modifying the ring search. He told people as he checked them out that if they found a wedding ring set in their purchase, they'd win a prize. More people searching made me happy. I heard Johnny offering to check inside the house for likely hiding places if Miss Lily didn't mind.

Johnny entered the house as Anna and Ellen returned, flushed and happy with their wedding attire. Then it was just a matter of settling on a price, with the women protesting that the wedding dress was worth much more than Miss Lily was asking, and she wanting to give them a discount to show her support. Eventually, she graciously accepted their offer and said she was having a BOGO sale, so the pantsuit was free. She'd be happy to hem the pants while they shopped.

I was getting ready to ask if they'd like an ABBA tribute band for the reception when the Parasol Protectors closed ranks and brought their weapons up in a defensive posture. It took the reenactors and Marjorie's singlestick students a little longer to hobble to the sidewalk. Those in Regency dress girded their loins by hiking their skirts and tying the lower edge around their waists, like ancient warriors. They too lined up and assumed a strike-ready position, as though Jane Austen and Conan the Barbarian had given birth to a female army.

Being tall has its advantages, like seeing over a crowd. Clustered near the curb, in front of the big tree where I'd stacked our pumpkins, stood a Texan's worst nightmare. Nine guys, including those who'd scoped us out earlier, each cradled a rifle. They wished they were still young. They all wore scraggly beards over tatty T-shirts and jeans, like a uniform. Defenders and shoppers outnumbered the gunners, but the AR-15s more than evened the field.

That broke me. Grandmothers arming themselves to shield their family, friends, kids, and dogs. The Protectors, turning out to defend the right of their friends to shop in safety. And me. I've always hated bullies. Before my eyes flashed every smaller, darker, weirder kid I'd stood up for; my little sisters; the women I'd walked home from the library and rescued from bad dates. That's what I thought about, marching forward while the rest of the shoppers took refuge behind the tables and food carts. I can't count the number of people who've asked me since then, "JD, what were you *thinking*?"

Toddlers wept, and an older child shushed them, saying, "You can't cry 'cause that tells them where you are."

Seeing fifty shades of red, I strode into the street and shouted in my best courtroom voice, "May I help you?"

The men exchanged puzzled glances. I guess my response wasn't what they were used to.

I glared from one to another. "You must need help, if you thought bringing guns to a Saturday morning yard sale was a good idea."

The leader scowled and jerked his gun into position. A quiet voice behind me said a single word in a language I didn't know.

Cupcake, a silent silver bullet, bounded forward, knocking me aside as she grabbed Mr. Big Man's trigger hand. Blood spurted. He screamed and dropped his rifle. Already stumbling from Cupcake's charge, I dropped lower and lunged forward to grab the gun. He was smart enough to have left the safety on, but that wouldn't matter if it hit the pavement. I backed up and set it on the ground, out of reach of its owner.

The dogs who'd followed Cupcake all morning, stealing kolaches and tacos, followed her into battle, baying. Good doggos one and all, they didn't break anyone's skin. I'm sure of it. They barked and growled as they pounced through the middle of the group. Some guy stumbled and raised his gun, more to get it out of the dogs' reach than to shoot. I charged back in and grabbed the firearm.

The confusion allowed the Parasol Protectors and Marjorie's singlestick troops to close in and apply their weapons, both pointed and flat. Officer Al gave more commands to Cupcake while he cuffed the men who fell. When Cupcake attached herself to a gun-toting hand, one of our team yanked the rifle away. She knew who the bad guys were. She hadn't been trained on sharpened parasols and elder canes.

A man at the back of the terrorists, the one who'd marched up and down the street earlier, yelled, "You can't do this in our town, you perverts."

From behind me, an aged voice quavered through Chantal's bullhorn. "Whose town, Jackson Byle? You're from Denton, Texas. Sleeping on my sofa for a month doesn't make you from Beauchamp. And Benny Preston, you should be ashamed of yourself, terrorizing our neighbors and friends. You'll be looking for a new place to live, because I'm not supporting this kind of behavior. You can pack your bags and go back to your mother's house or under a bridge, for all I care. Take your sleazy friend with you. I ain't cooking him one more meal."

Benny had to be the guy frozen in place with a stricken expression. He looked like the youngest in the group, probably mid-twenties. I'm not sure which was worse, being evicted or being called out by his grandmother in public.

"Shoot the durned dogs!" shouted one of the aggressors, swinging his arm at the German Shepherd.

Though the dog was built like a tank, he yipped in pain from the blow. An anguished voice behind me sobbed, "Ragnar!" The dog whined.

Seconds thereafter a nearby human screamed. A sideways glance told me Johnny had entered the fray with his martial arts skills. No way would he allow an animal to be hurt. Human animals were another issue.

Marjorie Feral bellowed to her troops. "We got their guns. Now aim for their balls!"

The few men still on their feet took off running. When they reached the tree, pumpkins rained from the branches. One knocked a man down. The rest of the vegetables splatted into orange goo. I gave a thumbs up to the kids in the tree.

With the field cleared, Johnny tried to examine the German Shepherd who'd cried. He didn't seem to be hurt, because he resumed dancing about with the other dogs after running up to his human for a hug. Cupcake led her canine brigade to the food carts. The grateful owners fed the hero dogs tacos, kolaches, pizza, and egg rolls.

Deputy Sheriff Clement pulled up and jumped out of his car. His wife Mindy reappeared and screeched, "It's about time you got here! I called you ages ago. These people are harassing me!"

"Mindy, shut up," he bellowed, like she was one of his perps.

My heart warmed to him. He was out of his jurisdiction, but he jumped in to lend a hand by cuffing the last few would-be shooters. While he and Officer Al consulted, Johnny and I carefully laid the rifles on a quilt after going through standard safety procedures.

Shouting, I ran toward the lawmen. "Everybody here is going to file charges against every one of those guys for all the damages in the world!"

While I threw around my legal weight, Johnny took the now-heavy gun-laden quilt across the street to Gregg House.

CHAPTER 4

SATURDAY AFTERNOON: THE HONOR OF YOUR PRESENCE

The shoulder-to-shoulder shopping crowd stood motionless, still in shock. The pastor-auctioneer started to offer a prayer of thanksgiving for our deliverance, but it dwindled to "thank you, thank you, thank you." The women on horseback lowered their shotguns, which I hadn't noticed before. We'd had even more protection than I thought.

When recovery started to set in, parents hugged their children and sobbed along with them, even the rough, tough, pumpkin brigade. Friends clustered together in group hugs, even Chantal and Darryl.

Ellen pulled Anna into her arms and declared, "I want to get married right now. We could die any minute, and I don't want to die before declaring publicly, legally, and every other way possible that I love you and commit all of myself and my life to you."

Anna, tears coursing down her cheeks, hugged her back. "Me too. But how?"

Chantal ascended into problem-solver mode, the best thing to get her back to normal. "We can do that. The sticking point, legally, is the license."

"We have a license," said Ellen. "We got it last month, but her parents…"

"…threw a fit, and we couldn't decide what to do," finished Anna.

"Anna wanted a big wedding, and I wanted her to have it, but without parents, a venue, and an officiant, we didn't know where to start," said Ellen.

I don't usually volunteer legal advice, but I was rattled too. "You've still got time to plan. The license is good for eighty-nine days."

Chantal clapped her hands. "We got this then. Parents? Who needs them? You have enough witnesses. Bridal party too. Venue? Right over there in the park next door in the gazebo. Officiant? Johnny's the assistant justice of the peace."

Johnny had returned with a handful of leashes and was clipping them onto the dogs who were not Cupcake. He looked up in alarm from Ragnar the German Shepherd, finally still enough for a quick exam, while his person, a slender man a few years older than me knelt by Ragnar's head and petted him. "I handle dead bodies. Not weddings. They're completely different things."

Chantal plowed on. "Well, JD then. He got himself declared a minister by one of those online churches of universal whatever, and he's married a bunch of our friends, gay people, unchurched people, whatever. He sounds all solemn and official in his courtroom voice. You up for this, JD? Your certification still good?"

"Well, I—"

"Okay then. I've got a robe from when I was in the Pride choir last summer. You can wear that so you'll look like you belong in a pulpit. The brides have their outfits."

The wedding couple and every other nearby woman put their heads together in a flurry of planning. I stepped away to avoid being assigned any more responsibility than I already had, just by opening my mouth once. After a few minutes, Chantal grabbed the bullhorn from the auctioneer and announced, "We're having a wedding. Everybody go get what you need and be back here in half an hour. JD, go get our music stuff."

After tending the dogs, Johnny went inside with Miss Lily to show her the results of his search.

When I caught up with him, he was gesturing to various containers on her dining room table. "I didn't want to go through your things, but I've set aside some possible hiding places."

She touched a silk-covered box with a small bouquet of silk flowers and ribbons on the top. "My Bible box! I made it for our family Bible and our wedding souvenirs. I haven't looked in it for so long. It's too painful since my husband died."

I pulled Johnny outside, and the two of us went into roadie mode. In short order, we had my keyboard, Johnny's viola and bass guitar, and our outdoor speakers loaded on the trailer behind the tractor, where the bride and bride sat in the oversized tractor seat. Chantal, transformed into a brown-skinned Agnetha with long blonde locks, staggered across the street under an armload of wedding paraphernalia, including, I was sorry to see, a choir robe of many colors—at least ten shades in diagonal stripes—for me. After a few minutes, another brown-skinned, blonde Agnetha limped across the street, while pulling on high heels. The Parasol Protectors cheered.

I raised my eyebrows. "Well, well. If it isn't Miss Swannie Chalant."

Early in his tenure with Black Orchid Enterprises, Darryl displayed his light falsetto soprano, and we recruited him for the band as a backup soprano when Chantal sang with us and substituting for her when she had a gig elsewhere. She put him in touch with the drag community to turn him into a more convincing woman. Darryl's only stipulation, once he was dressed like a soprano, was that he not perform in the Beauchamp area where he was born and bred. Here he was in a yellow bandage dress and high heels, just like, or mostly like Chantal, showing Miss Swannie to the whole town. He fell into the embrace of the Protectors until Johnny and Chantal extended their hands to him and pulled him into the trailer.

Although we could see the gazebo from Miss Lily's yard, driving the equipment around the block to the parking lot made setup easier. Those who could walked toward the park, each carrying two folding chairs.

The horsewomen rode ahead toward Main Street. The Parasol Protectors marched in formation behind the trailer. I hooked up my keyboard and played "Dancing Queen" for them. They cheered and went into a dance routine, completely G-rated. Behind them, the other tractor and trailer carried Marjorie's singlestick brigade, Miss Lily, and other mobility-challenged patrons. Marjorie's women twirled their canes like batons. As a former marching band player (trombone), I winced in expectation of batons thrown up in the air and coming down on, say, for instance, the trombone section. Fortunately, no one tossed their canes while I was watching. With age (sometimes) comes wisdom.

Trundling down Louisiana Street, we could see Main Street, blocked off for the morning's parade, consisting of the high school marching band, a couple of local business floats, and Santa Claus. A very short event.

The horsewomen pushed the orange barrier cones aside and led us into the parade behind Santa. Then I saw the rest of the parade, the Guadalupe girls and guy, including our own Guadalupe Dianne Cortez, forming up behind us and throwing soft fabric red roses into the crowd. Maybe Father Emilio hadn't wanted them too close to secularity. I wondered how he felt about them following the drag queen dance group, not to mention the bridal pair waving from the tractor seat.

The parade made its way through downtown, looped through the elementary school parking lot, and then headed down the next street over. We pulled into the park's parking lot. To my surprise, so did the two Guadalupe floats.

Father Emilio took over the gazebo as his Guadalupes filed into a semicircle in front of him. Except for the man, who went by the name of Lupe, and the baby in her mother's arms, they all carried bouquets of silk red roses. Baby Guadalupe had a rose embroidered on her blue-starred onesie and a rose plushie that she clutched in a baby death grip. The part of the town who hadn't attended Miss Lily's yard sale gathered respectfully at a distance. Our people wandered in too, setting up their chairs in expectation of a wedding.

The area by the gazebo was a nice, open space for a gathering. Also for a shooting, if the would-be gunmen from this morning had friends. I glanced around, taking in the mostly one-story residences. I could see the two-story downtown buildings, where the windows or roofs might conceal a sniper. They didn't, as far as I could tell. Not yet.

I didn't hear the sermon because I was lugging music paraphernalia into place. I didn't hear much of the short speeches from the namesakes, but I held up my phone to record what Guadalupe Dianne

Cortez had to say about what her name meant to her. I wanted Dianne to show her mother how involved she was with the local church.

"I adopted my middle name in college," she said. "Although my family still calls me 'Lupita.' I just got sick of a lifetime of hearing Guadalupe weaponized into Looney Lupita, Little Latin Loopy Lou, and other products of evil childish imagination. Nevertheless, I am proud to bear the name of Mexico's patron saint and strive to uphold the ideals Our Lady represents for us all.

"My siblings are also named for shrines to the Virgin. Of course, we all studied our own and each other's stories, from which I learned that our Blessed Mother appears not to the rich, not to the powerful, but to the poor, ill, and suffering. To women, children, indigenous. She can come to you anywhere in any guise, like a heavenly Barbie."

She said another sentence or two, but those were drowned out by the crowd, cheering with glee for their heavenly Barbie. A ghost of a smile flickered Father Emilio's face too.

After Father Emilio's final blessing, the wedding crew moved in. Chantal brought Dianne up to speed, and as they collected the blue capes (for next year's parade), asked the Guadalupes, now clad in long, pale red dresses, to serve as attendants. One woman had to get back home for the babysitter but left her dress for Chantal. Once she understood what was happening, a mother of an eight-year-old Guadalupe, grabbed her child by the hand and marched off, spewing homophobia all the way.

Pro tip: If you're going to drag your child out of an event in protest, don't stick around. This mother went to upbraid Father Emilio. When little Guadalupe realized other people were getting a privilege she wasn't, she responded with ear-splitting shrieks. Miss Lily went to her with the precious Bible box in hand and showed it to the child but addressed the mother. "Would you consent to her carrying my family Bible down the aisle to the…" She looked at me askance. "…priest."

Askance was warranted. Not only did my vestments sport bright diagonal stripes, but Chantal was five-foot-nothing to my six-foot-three. Her robe, long on her, almost reached my knees. It covered my grubby cargo shorts, but not my bare legs and Birks, not the norm for pulpits or lecterns. I wear pastel satin suits and body suits in an ABBA tribute band, so I don't freak out over clothing, but today's outfit stretched the limits of my tolerance.

I'd be reading the service from my phone, and it didn't include Bible verses, but Miss Lily smiled at me and said, "In the Bible is the wedding service from my husband's and my wedding. It would mean a lot to me if you'd use that. I talked to Ellen and Anna, and they're fine with it."

Alrighty then. I smiled and nodded. I was willing to try for Miss Lily's sake and the sake of little Guadalupe, who gave her mother a trembling smile through tears.

I was going to say something, but at that moment, Father Emilio and Kevin Dixon, justice of the peace, approached me. Kevin had pulled on a jacket over his Sonic Drive-In shirt, where he's the franchise owner and manager.

Kevin looked concerned. "JD, Johnny called to tell me about this wedding. They can have anyone they want to conduct their ceremony, but I'm not sure why they asked Johnny, who really didn't want to and never has done so before, instead of me."

"Chantal put this together," I responded.

"Oh, I see. Chantal."

"Yes, Chantal. I think the original issue was that they weren't sure you'd conduct an LGBTQ+ ceremony."

He raised his eyebrows in shock. "I'd conduct a ceremony for anyone with a license. It's the law of the land."

I brightened. "Glad to hear it. I'll ask them if they'd rather have you."

He looked down. "My cousin's gay, but he's never actually told me. I'd like him to know I'm okay with it. And other gay people who'd like to get married."

Father Emilio, tall and spare, added, "Would you ask them also whether they'd like me to say a prayer for them in the service?"

I shut my surprised, gaping mouth with a snap. "You can do that?"

He drew himself up to his full height, just about eye level with me. "I'm not in church. I'm not the officiant. I would hope I can offer prayers for whomever I please."

"I'd hope so too, but I wouldn't count on it. I'll ask." I shuffled over to where the brides waited to walk down the aisle.

They stood by the edge of the parking lot and brushed hay from each other's outfits. Anna exclaimed, "Oh, we want you to do the ceremony. You were the first to say yes."

Not exactly true, but it was nice to be wanted. Maybe.

Ellen ran her fingers through her short curls. "Maybe the JP could do part of the ceremony, just to show people he's willing. Same for the priest, if you don't mind, Anna. Let people see them standing up for us."

I added, when Anna hesitated, "It's your wedding. You don't have to save the world on your special day."

Her face broke into smiles. "If not now, when? Tell them we'd love to have their blessings."

"As long as it's a good blessing," added Ellen, suddenly cautious.

After I confirmed with the JP and the priest, I sat down at my keyboard, now moved to the gazebo, for this multitasking event. I played a few opening arpeggios, like Bach's Prelude No. 1 that serves as the accompaniment for the Gounod "Ave Maria."

You're probably not interested in my musical arrangements.

Johnny, who'd been warming up on his viola, began a slow, stately version of ABBA's "My Love, My Life" to guide the wedding party down the sidewalk aisle to the gazebo. His eyes kept flickering to the downtown buildings. My eyes followed his to the rooftops and second story windows that might conceal gunmen.

The Guadalupe bridesmaids came first, with their silk rose bouquets. The Bible box bearer came next, a proud look on her little face while she marched in front of the brides.

I didn't know what to do. I should receive the Bible box from the child, and all I could think to do was hold one hand out while I continued playing with the other hand. Miss Swannie saved the day by stepping in front of the lectern and accepting the box with as low a bow as she could make in a bandage dress.

Miss Lily held an arm of each bride and marched them to the lectern/altar. The Protectors, Marjorie's crew, and older Guadalupes, including Mr. Lupe, followed the brides. I detected Dianne's hand in the Mexican custom of madrinas and padrinos who provide support for the wedding in some way, usually financial. Today these attendants acted like fairy godmothers and godfathers, offering blessings and good wishes while the security teams encircled the event. The horsewomen patrolled the parking lot. A lump swelled in my throat because they felt they had to guard their friends even at their wedding. I glanced again at the roofs and windows and once again caught Johnny doing the same. Officer Al and Cupcake crossed into the park from Miss Lily's house. Both made me feel safer.

When everyone stopped moving, I had to start the service. I left the safety of my keyboard and took the lectern. Hoping it contained the wedding service I needed, I opened the Bible box. If Miss Lily was to be believed, it was the first time anyone had opened it for months, maybe longer, as crusty as the hinges were.

I riffled the Bible's pages and ran my hand around its edges in search of the service. I hit the jackpot twice. The service booklet, yellow with age, was tucked in the Bible's ancestry pages. And I pulled out something else from the box, something hard and lumpy, hidden by the Bible's edges. I opened my hand to reveal two white gold rings, one a plain band, one with a chip diamond.

Ellen made circles with one hand, encouraging me to get going.

I cleared my throat. "Dearly beloved, we are gathered here today… for many reasons. But when love called, we answered. I hope we'll live the rest of our lives that way." I wandered back to the standard version, which you've probably heard. Dianne and Chantal sang "My Love, My Life," slightly adjusted for a wedding. Father Emilio gave them the standard Biblical blessing of "May the Lord bless you and keep you, etc." Anna and Ellen read poems they'd written for each other. We had vows, rings, and Miss Lily doing double mother duty and sniffling in the first row of the congregation. Kevin took over after the vows so I could get back to the keyboard and play the bridal party out under an arch of canes and parasols.

I sighed in relief as I scanned the roofs, windows, and the surrounding area one last time.

After we played and sang a rousing rendition of "I Do, I Do, I Do, I

Do, I Do," I found Miss Lily and folded the rings into her hand. Her sniffles broke down into sobs.

She returned the rings to her finger and clutched her hand as though to keep them there forever.

Another scene played out nearby while I patted her back in efforts at comfort. Miss Doria pushed her way to where Swannie/Darryl, Chantal, and Dianne were moving the band equipment forward to set up for the reception.

Miss Doria reached up with both hands and pinched his cheeks as she thundered, "Isn't my grandson the best singer? Dancer too. Why have you kept all this talent hidden?"

"Aw, Granny." His voice wandered between Swannie and Darryl. "I didn't want—I thought you—I didn't want you to be ashamed of me."

"No tears, Swannie. Remember the makeup," called Chantal.

The resulting snort was closer to Darryl.

Miss Doria placed her hands on his shoulders. "Darryl—is it Swannie? Have you ever done drugs? Been arrested?"

"No! Not even a speeding ticket. Might have had a beer, maybe. And someone gave me a gummy once, might have had something in it."

"Joined a gang?"

"No! Not that they'd want me, but the feeling's mutual."

She kissed his cheek. "Then, honey, if all you want to do is prance around being fabulous, I am purely relieved and I'll buy you makeup for Christmas."

"Really? There's this line that's perfect for Black skin, but it's so expensive. Oh, Granny, thank you!

She patted his cheek. "Honey, I sewed lace ruffles on your pink homecoming tux. I've been waiting for you to tell me your pronouns."

"As soon as I decide, I'll let you know. K?"

EPILOGUE

I admit the reception went on longer than most. Parties last as long as the music and food hold out. Once members of the Parasol Protectors volunteered to sing, they turned the event into karaoke, giving MultiABBA's voices lots of breaks. Later we turned the music over to the local DJs who showed up. Then Darryl and I set up a passworded website for everyone's wedding photos and videos, which inspired people to take and upload more.

The restaurant carts kept serving until their evening hours started. Mary Chang's wedding cake, a tower of white iced and coconut donuts was a nice touch. People wandered from the yard sale to the reception and back again, fueled by the constant food and drink.

I sighed down to the center of the earth when the door closed behind me back home at Gregg House. Mostly it had been a happy day, but a day of constant vigilance.

The sale brought Miss Lily over $35,000, between her farm equipment and antique furniture. I don't know how much she had left after she went around to the day's helpers and pressed large wads of cash on them, but Chantal was thrilled with what she received.

Miss Lily is still selling her house, even though Mindy Clement apologized to everyone and dropped her HOA campaign after Deputy Clement and I talked. Miss Lily and the other neighbors are considering whether to continue their lawsuit. Miss Lily is moving into the cottage on Anna and Ellen's property while she decides what she wants to do, thereby avoiding a winter in Chicago.

After eating everything in sight, Cupcake and Ragnar staggered home with their owners, and Johnny brought the stray hero dogs to the Gregg House shelter. Beauchampians can adopt them for a nominal fee. You can see them on our website, along with the new information that I can conduct weddings.

It's absolutely not true that we refuse to return the rifles. Believing they were part of a police case, Johnny secured them in Gregg House and turned them over to the police, who turned them over to the county, who sent them back in one of their typical jurisdictional squabbles. When neither county nor city decided to pursue criminal charges, Johnny collected the rifles and took them to an Austin dealer to look them over and make sure they weren't damaged. It's a busy time of year, so I don't expect them back until after our open house.

I think the gun owners are fine with that, though. The guy from Denton left town, run out of this one, you might say. Johnny invited the others to his usual Friday night community dinner, along with Marjorie and the Parasol Protectors, in disguise as regular guys. The gunmen left shortly after gulping down a plate or two of Johnny's delicacies, but I figure it's a start in building bridges.

They almost stayed to play poker, but they bailed when Marjorie picked up the cards to deal. Maybe it's best they left. The drill captain cleaned us all out and then did a victory dance, straight from Broadway, with the other Protectors joining in a fine chorus line.

After poker, the rest of us had a good time decking the halls for the open house, wrapping presents, and singing carols around the piano. We turned on the air-conditioning so we could light a fire, as you do in Texas. We huddled up to drink cocoa, eat peppermint-chocolate cookies, and pretend it was winter. Good times.

And that's the way I remember it, Harry. Of course, you know how unreliable eyewitness testimony is. Merry Christmas to you too.

PART THREE

BE IT RESOLVED

CHAPTER 1

I made a New Year's resolution to supervise the office better. Not the individual companies; Johnny Ly runs his cat veterinary clinic however the cats will let him, and I'd never presume to tell Dianne Cortez how to run anything, least of all her accountancy office. I, JD Thompson, can handle my own law office. I fill out wills for people with nothing to leave, caution people that shooting their irritating neighbor does not qualify for the Stand Your Ground defense, and do immigration work for nonprofits, but Black Orchid Enterprises is greater than the sum of its parts, and somebody (me, because the others are busy) needs to keep it on track—especially our intern, a local community college student whom we acquired in one of our earliest adventures. (See "The Way Old Friends Do," *Birth of the Black Orchids*)

Darryl Swann cheerfully scoops litter boxes between filling out simple tax forms and standard law paperwork while he answers the phone and keeps Black Orchid Enterprises social media alive, a task Johnny, Dianne, and I hate.

We funnel him tidbits to post about tax due dates, spay and neuter clinics, pet adoption and health, and points of law relevant to the average citizen. We even give him our ABBA tribute band performance dates and family photos for Throwback Thursday—anything rather than leave Darryl to his creative devices. We still remember his Passover-Easter promotion.

Even though late February was long past time to abandon New Year's resolutions, I signed into our social media accounts instead of just skimming the public side. I sighed.

"Darryl," I called over his typing and humming the soprano background to "Thank You for the Music," "Who's Sgt. Theodore Baldrick? Why is Miss Swannie Chalant talking to him?"

Darryl stopped humming but kept on typing. "Teddy Boy? Just this dude I'm chatting with. And Miss Swannie Chalant is also my *nom de net* as well as my MultiABBA band name. She's just taking out the internet trash. What do you think?"

"I think you're on the company clock. Miss Swannie can chat with buff military dudes on her own time."

"He slid into my DMs with a nasty photo. I was just getting rid of him."

Disgusted with my fellow men, I shook my head. "Does that happen often? I don't want you working in a hostile environment."

"It don't bother me. If women can work social media with all the gross pics and death threats, I can too. Miss Swannie definitely knows how to handle them."

I would have replied, but Dianne pinged me, asking me to come to her office. As I walked across the gallery past his desk, I said, "Just block, report, and move on."

"No fun," he mumbled.

I bet you're ready for an explanation. Ten years ago, University of Texas college student Chantal Gaumont (double major in accounting and music) put together an ABBA tribute band from things lying around the house, namely her roommates Dianne (alto voice, accounting major), Johnny (tenor, bass player, pre-vet), and JD (me, bass-baritone, keyboardist, pre-law). We thrilled audiences and filled our pocketbooks through grad school.

Three of us assumed we'd grow up and get real jobs after graduation. Part of that was right, about the real jobs, but Chantal is determined to be a professional singer, and Dianne's mother is an event planner, so we keep singing, whether we want to or not. (We want to.)

So far, our growing up process has led us to chuck the jobs, but not the band, and open the loosely connected firm of Black Orchid Enterprises in Johnny's ancestral mansion in the middle of Texas and nowhere. The gargantuan Victorian pile with two turrets and wrap-around porches fits in the tatty little town as well as an alien spaceship, but it's a great house, big enough for our offices on the first floor and residences on the second.

Darryl, or Miss Swannie, got involved because Chantal is becoming a successful (read: booked, even recorded) musician in her own right. When Mrs. Cortez books a gig, usually a quinceañera, on top of Chantal's obligations, we perform with Darryl's tuneful falsetto in her place. His voice isn't strong enough to carry the melody, but Dianne can lead the alto-melody songs with the rest of us warbling background vocals.

In her gleaming, chrome-and-glass office, Dianne looked at me with tragic eyes, her Dolorosa expression. She has the same expression when we run out of Diet Pepsi, so I always wait before panicking. "I need your help."

"For what?" I asked, sinking into one of her spindly client chairs. It looks like something from Barbie's Dream Office. I'm never convinced it's going to hold my weight.

"My aunt. My cousin, actually. Do you remember my mother's cousin Soledad? I call her tía—"

"You call every female relative tía who's at least ten years older than you. Excuse me if I can't keep them all straight."

"It's the custom. She's six years older than my mother and the daughter of Mamí's Tía Pilar—"

"Is this going to be on the test? Because I doubt if I could recognize people outside your immediate family, unless they did something bizarre in my presence. Also, this story is wandering around like the Candyland board."

She tapped a stylus on the clear desktop. "My Tío Juan asked me to manage her money after he died—that was last year—and I did as he asked. She quit work when he got sick, and then she was too distraught to do anything. So I invested most of the insurance payout, arranged for monthly payments to her account, and put her bills on autopay. I told her to let me know if she needed more, like for big expenses. She told me she wanted to lend $10,000 to a friend. I said no, the money's for her, not her friends, and it's my job to protect her money." Dianne wiggled in her chair.

"Let me guess. She wanted to buy bitcoin or NFTs?"

"She doesn't even know what those are. She's been chatting with men online, men who wanted her to send them money."

I sat up straighter. "And she did?"

"Yes, small amounts at first, but then she needed more. She told me about her romance, and I…I wasn't sympathetic. A month later, she says she needs $8,000 to repair her roof. I sent my father and Tío Pedro to look at it. Her roof is perfectly fine. Words were said, her final words to me, she claimed, when I invited her to sue me because I wouldn't give her money to send to her Nigerian prince."

"It's Ghana these days," I said.

"Whichever. Then I hear she's gone back to work as a classroom assistant at the local elementary school. That's progress, right? Except she did it so that she'll have more money to send to Prince Vapor. I want to sue this ladrón who robbed her."

"Last I heard, that's a crime, and the police can take care of it. For free."

She slumped like a deflated balloon. "She willingly gave it to him when he said he needed it for his sister's school fees or his mother's cancer, maybe both. Lies, of course."

"That's sad, but not illegal. I mean, not enforceable. Once the funds go overseas, it's a black hole, as far as getting your money back. Nigeria and Ghana have no interest in helping us."

If possible, her expression grew even more tragic.

I said in a soft voice, "Dianne, if I could do anything, I would. This guy is beyond our reach. She might as well have thrown the money off the Colorado River Bridge. At least you've preserved the greater part of her assets. Unless you can have her declared incompetent, she's free to spend her salary however she likes."

Dianne turned away. "Incompetent isn't the same as stupid."

CHAPTER 2

The next day, when I brought back lunch from the Happy Family Restaurant, Dianne yelled from her office, "JD, can we use that photo of you dancing at my cousin's wedding?"

"Sure," I said on autopilot as I danced around four kittens swarming me or the open door; I'm not sure which.

I set the bag of community egg rolls and won ton soup on the front desk and went to my own office. I answered three emails before my sense of self-preservation kicked in.

Dianne and Chantal sat with their laptops open on the far side of Dianne's glass worktable. Despite ancestries from opposite sides of the globe, they looked like my twin sisters caught in the act of something, their eyes wide and shoulders hunched. Something told me Dianne didn't want my picture for the company social media. Chantal was helping Dianne with the upcoming flood of tax work, but she didn't need my photo for that.

Officer Al, formally known as Officer Alejandro Quintanilla-Villanueva, sat near the door. He swallowed his egg roll and replied with all the aplomb a young, recently minted officer can muster, "Dianne and Chantal are helping me with my inquiries."

"Oh? Am I part of a lineup?" I asked.

Chantal, earnest as a nun, said, "Not like that at all! No one will recognize you."

I picked up Dianne's white and gold cat Nevada from the last chair in the room and put her in my lap. "Obviously there's a story."

They shared glances. Chantal turned her laptop around so I could see her graphics work.

It doesn't often happen, but I was struck silent.

"I blended you with this Spanish soccer star." She opened another photo. "I couldn't use him—"

"Because everyone would say, 'That's Fernando Torres,'" I said. "So why have you joined Fernando and me in this unholy Photoshop-imony? Though we do look…is *dashing* the word? If older."

"I was going for silver fox," said Chantal. "Though still somewhat golden."

"Something to aspire to," I agreed. "Why do you need a silver-gold fox?"

Glances flew around the room again, an undertow of things unsaid.

Dianne sighed. "I see we're going to have to tell you everything."

I smiled and stretched my legs. The office felt cramped with four people in it, not to mention four kittens. Two tabbies, brown and orange, wrestled across Dianne's keyboard. Another tabby slashed at ankles from under the desk.

"Officer Alejandro has a case like my tía, a lady who invested money in an online romance."

He nodded. "The financial detectives in the Austin Police Department are investigating an international crime network, and one of the victims lives in Beauchamp. I talked to her, and she insisted that they and I were lying. She knew this man loved her and would come here to join her, as soon as he paid off debts and bribed officials for a visa. She sent him $12,000. He was more real to her than me, sitting in the same room with her. She'd never do anything to hurt him. What do you do when the biggest obstacle is the victim?"

Chantal declared, "Well, we're doing something about it." She gestured to her laptop. "Meet Diego García Aznar."

"Don't show him to my mother," Dianne said. "She'll have me engaged to him in a week."

"Don't show him to my dad," I replied. "He'll think it's his long-lost son."

Chantal mused, "I think we should send him to JD's dad and see what he'll pay for Diego never to show up on the doorstep as his son."

"I think you should remember I'm an officer of the court and Al is an officer of the law," I advised. "And that my father's also a lawyer, a bad choice for scams."

"I'm joking." But she eyed Al hard, to make sure he knew.

Officer Al forced a grin. "JK, right. The photo does look a lot like JD."

"Him and that Spanish soccer star. But older. You think your aunt will go for him, Dianne?"

Dianne said, "For certain. Crop the other people out, though. She'd recognize our relatives."

"K. What do you think of this dude?" Chantal displayed a hand-some, middle-aged Black guy with distinguished close-cropped silver hair.

"Not my type," I said.

Dianne scolded, "Seriously, Chantal. Why ask *him*?"

"Well, what about you?"

"If I had Daddy issues, maybe. But I saw you put him together: Barack Obama, Denzel Washington, and Random Black Guy from Photostock."

Chantal turned to the policeman. "What do you think, Officer? Will your victim like him?"

"Just what are you planning to do?" he asked, alarmed.

"Nothing illegal. We checked with our attorney."

"Now wait a minute," I objected, trying to remember.

"You said it wasn't illegal to use another identity if you weren't committing crimes. I'm just creating a social media profile to send friend requests to scam-prone women. Officer Al said divorcées and widows over fifty, though any woman-looking person gets requests like that every day. Maybe they'll like Diego García Aznar and Javonte DeKeyser better than the usual scumbuckets."

"Really?" exclaimed the policeman. "Every day?"

Dianne and Chantal nodded.

I added, "I get such requests too, but from nubile young women in Russia, Eastern Europe, Asia, all willing to marry me or join whatever arrangement I desire if I send them money to come to the States. Knowing that they're really guys in huts working for a syndicate helps me resist. What happens next, Chantal?"

She lifted a shoulder. "Online romances never go anywhere, not if they stay online. We'll encourage our girlfriends to go out, meet people, like bowling or church potlucks or whatever old ladies do."

Dianne said, "They'll meet real guys or join quilting clubs and won't need imaginary lovers anymore."

Squirming on top of his spindly chair, Officer Al said, "I didn't tell you her name."

Chantal's lips gradually stretched. The ends turned up. "No, but if I slide my way into Beauchamp groups, I'll find her or someone similar."

I raised my hands in defeat and returned to my office.

Al followed me. "Aren't you going to do something?"

"I resolved long ago to stay out of their way unless they were planning something actionable. Otherwise, they're free to screw up however they like. I first lived with them in college, and once I asked for a house rule that everyone wear socially approved underwear— bras— in the common areas. That earned me a slide show and lecture from Dianne, and Chantal made me an underwired jockstrap to give me some empathy for their sufferings."

"Wow."

I shrugged. "I was young."

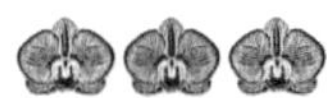

Ever since college, Johnny has fixed a big dinner on Friday nights. In Beauchamp, Officer Al and half of the town show up. As we gathered around the table, Chantal and Dianne looked like cats with a canary.

"It's going great," said Chantal, not that anybody asked. "I've met a bunch of ladies online. We're setting up nights out for seniors at the rec center and local restaurants."

"How is that going to work?" I asked.

"Obviously I'm not going. Javonte will have a problem at the last minute. Car won't start or something. They'll have fun without me."

Officer Al frowned. "I don't like it. It's deceitful. Nobody's ever used a fake name for a good reason."

"That's not fair," argued Chantal. "Performers and artists do it all the time."

"Sure," said Officer Al. "That's for their protection."

"Or their brand," said Chantal. "Me, I have a perfect name for a singer. If my name were Edna Galumph, I'd have to change it."

"That would be for your benefit. No one changes their name to help anybody else." Officer Al turned red.

Dianne turned thoughtful. "What about Camilla?"

"Right," Chantal agreed. "Like Angela or Angel Shots."

Officer Al looked more confused than ever.

Chantal sighed. "Guess you don't have that out here in the sticks. You should. If your date is sus, you ask the bartender if Angela's working tonight, or you order an Angel Shot. The bartender calls you a rideshare so you can sneak out. Sometimes there's a sign in the bathroom about it."

Dianne nodded, her eyes haunted. "Camilla's a local version of that. I met a date for the first time at a bar. Five minutes in, I excused myself and ran out the back door to my car. The tires were slashed. I ran back inside to the bathroom. A card on the mirror said, 'Feel unsafe? Call Camilla.' I stayed there until 'Camilla' texted me from the back parking lot. Camilla's this big dude, like the guy in *Moana*—at least seven feet tall, hair bushing out. I don't want to get in his car, and I sure don't want to tell him where I live.

"He says, 'I know you're scared. Here's some choices: You dial 911 and keep your finger on the call button while I drive. You call a friend and stay on the phone with her until I drop you off. I can take you to a police station, a mall, any place you feel safe. Or you can walk somewhere, and I'll follow you, real slow. Your call, but I'm not sure how long you've got to decide.'

"It was pouring down rain. The bar's backdoor handle rattled behind me. I jumped in the car, and he took me someplace, no problem. He explained how his sister was murdered by a new boyfriend, so he wants to keep other women from the same fate." Dianne fell into a reverie.

Expressions ranged from appalled disbelief (the men) to sadly sympathetic (the women).

I knew the rest of the story. Later that night Dianne banged on the door of the sleek, boxy apartment I rented after I passed the bar. Soaked and dripping, she asked through chattering teeth if she could sleep on my sofa. She did, after taking a hot shower and donning one of the pajamas and robe sets that my grandmother keeps giving me. When we went to change the tires on her car the next day, we found it beat up with a hammer. Dianne filed a police report, but nothing ever came of it; all the information she thought she had about the guy was false. Camilla wasn't the only one with a fake identity, just the one with benign intentions.

"How often does this happen?" Officer Al's tentative voice broke the silence.

Her eyes wide and sad, Chantal ventured, "You quit keeping track, you know?"

I offered, "When we were in college, one of my housemates would call me about once a month to pick her up from a bad date."

In the following weeks, Dianne's expressions changed from satisfied to hunted, like the final weeks of a course with a major paper due. Chantal bailed after a few days, saying she had new respect for those guys overseas who sit in their huts all day and seduce money out of American women.

"You can't say it isn't hard work," she declared. "At least it takes a lot of time, time I don't have, if I'm going to get my album out this month. I've got to prepare for the last recording session."

We knew about the album. We'd contributed funds to it on every gift-giving occasion for a year. Some of us might be a birthday or two ahead.

Dianne persevered, having a personal stake. She brought her laptop to the breakfast table, a plausible time for Spain to communicate with the U.S. Her cousin still managed to get in a few replies, though she was at work. After work, Tía Soledad wanted to have long conversations with her beau, so Dianne dragged her laptop to the dinner table.

A few weeks later, she announced at lunch—tamales from Mama

Ana's truck, served at our breakfast nook table—that she'd found a way out.

Fingers flying across her keyboard, Dianne declared, "I'm changing his page to a memorial. So sad, Diego García Aznar dying unexpectedly."

"I should kill off Javonte too, just to make it final for them," said Chantal as she weighed her tamale. She works hard to control her diabetes. The rest of us appreciate it after that time we rushed her to the hospital. After cutting her allowable portion into tiny pieces, she returned to her laptop, alternating bites between typing. "Huh. That's weird. I can't log in." She worked at it a few more minutes before giving up.

I knew better, but I asked, "Them?"

"Oh, I talked to a lot of women in the online group for Alvarez County seniors, the Silver Panthers. I didn't ever show up at the group gatherings, obviously, but they look like they're having fun in the photos and videos they post. And it's all because Javonte started organizing it."

"You're a real public benefactor, just like Johnny," said Dianne, still typing away.

Johnny no sooner arrived in Beauchamp than he volunteered to be Assistant Animal Control Officer and Assistant Justice of the Peace. Both have added excitement to our lives, what with wrangling wild hogs, bobcats, and all the stray cats in the world for one job and pronouncing people dead for the other job.

Thinking back over all that excitement, I heaved a secret sigh of relief that nothing worse happened with Chantal's meetings.

CHAPTER 3

The following week took me to the Texas border for immigration cases. I returned home just in time to go with Johnny on a justice of the peace call. The local elected JP, also manager of a drive-in restaurant, doesn't like the death part of the job. He handles small claims court and weddings and lets Johnny declare people dead and determine the need for further investigation. Johnny being Johnny, he always thinks further investigation is needed, just to make sure. He likes me to go along as a buffer against law enforcement and their budget.

This scene of the crime was in Beauchamp proper, so the Beauchamp police would be in charge instead of the Alvarez County sheriff. The house sat in the older part of town, which describes most of it—the kind of house that the owner is relieved to have and hopes will last her lifetime.

Sadly, her hopes were realized. The house was obviously the victim's retirement plan. A woman in her sixties, she raised her children and lived with her husband in this dingy frame house.

Not wanting to see the carnage, I stayed on the front steps. I smiled and nodded at the neighbors: (1) an elderly lady pretending to garden while craning her neck to see the official proceedings and (2) a long-haired, bearded man walking on the opposite sidewalk and pretending not to be just as interested as the faux gardener. It's a Southern thing, acknowledging everyone you see, as though they're your besties. Otherwise, you look suspicious, like you don't belong.

Officer Al emerged from the house to mark the crime scene with evidence flags. "What did Chantal call her fantasy guy?"

"Javonte DeKeyser," I said. "But she quit him weeks ago. She wanted to declare him dead and set up a digital memorial, but she couldn't get back in. Probably lost the password."

Officer Al leaned over to set a flag beside a piece of card. From where I was, it looked like a torn business card. Someone had written on it in thick marker, but just the letters NM showed. "Mrs. Kelly's calendar said that Javonte DeK was bringing her lunch today." He set another flag by a cigarette butt.

"Chantal isn't *that* good with makeup." I gestured to the torn card. "If that card is important, it completely knocks her out of the picture."

Al's mouth dropped open. "Maybe it isn't, but we have to mark it as potential evidence. Why do you say that?"

I reveled in my Sherlock moment. I'm more used to playing Watson to Johnny's Great Detective. "You see, Officer, this card is clearly from the Nordic Nights bar."

"You can't see the whole name."

"No, but I see 'Nordic' in big fat letters with icicles dripping off— their brand. I see their logo, a line drawing of some chisel-jawed guy in the Arctic. Nordic Nights is a white club for white guys and their white girls, and there's no way a Black person would go there, especially Chantal. Years ago she found herself booked there in a colossal misunderstanding. She called an emergency performance of MultiABBA so she wouldn't be alone. She set up the stage so it looked like I was the soloist with my POC backup singers. I sang 'Does Your Mother Know' and songs from ABBA's first album, when the guys used to sing melody. Mostly I sang 'La la laaaaaah' and 'oompahpah oompahpah' like that was the tune. Even more amazing, nobody seemed to notice. Believe me, neither Chantal nor any other Black person would willingly set foot in Nordic Nights."

"What do you think NM means?" asked Al, pointing to the fat blue letters.

"No idea. Part of a password?"

We both shrugged. I watched him set evidence flags around the front yard. "Postage stamp" was a generous description of its size, and I wouldn't have called it trashy, but soon a field of merry yellow flags flapped in the late winter breeze and marked the yard's detritus. Crime scene workers have to mark anything out of place, even if they suspect it came from an overturned garbage can.

Officer Al was taking photos of his work when Johnny emerged from the house.

"It seems clear that she was murdered, strangled," Johnny said.

I raised an eyebrow. He'd taken a long time for a straightforward determination.

On the way home, he explained, "I made a copy of her computer to study later. The Beauchamp police force doesn't have an IT expert."

I could've pointed out that he wasn't one either, but any of the Black Orchids would have been more qualified than any of the police. And once Johnny decides to study something, he becomes an expert in short order.

Most of the time, one visit ends Johnny's involvement with a police case, though he's been known to unofficially advise. Officer Al owes one of his promotions to Johnny's help.

We returned to our normal duties, which now included getting Chantal to her recording session the next day. But the police chief requested her presence at the police station, bright and early (defined as before noon for Chantal). She politely declined, because she had to be at the recording studio soon. It would take months to get a new time, and she'd have to pay her session musicians anyway.

The police and her attorney explained that it wasn't a request. When the police want to talk to you, they do. You might get out of it for a funeral (your own) or having a baby, but I wouldn't count on the latter.

Shortly after we moved to Beauchamp, Assistant Animal Control Officer Johnny and his assistant—me—removed a bobcat from downtown. (The bobcat is fine, living in a nearby sanctuary.) I'd rather do that again than take Chantal in for police questioning. I told her to shut up unless I said otherwise, but that didn't mean she couldn't bristle and scowl when silent and speak in the voice of doom when allowed.

The Beauchamp Police Chief was convinced that Chantal lured Mrs. Elizabeth Kelly to her death, based on testimony of her calendar for the morning she died—"Javonte DeK bring lunch." I'm not sure whose jaw dropped lower, Chantal's or mine.

"Javonte doesn't exist except online," I managed after an eon. "Chantal hasn't logged on as him for some weeks." I didn't bother denying her connection when Officer Al knew all about it.

"I can't log in!" exclaimed Chantal.

In a firmer voice, I said, "She has an alibi for the time in question, no one in Mrs. Kelly's neighborhood has ever seen her there, and I personally doubt that she could physically have committed the murder. Nor can I imagine why."

"Ha!" said the chief. "How do you know what time she needs an alibi?"

"I don't. I do know she has been with someone in our house for every moment of every day except for personal hygiene. With tax season looming, the accountants won't have time even for sleep. I also imagine that ISP and other IT evidence will clear her."

Officer Al, acting as assistant, notetaker, and coffee bringer, looked miserable. The chief's face turned red as the Christmas ornaments we took down on January 6. Same shape too. He decided he needed to hear every detail of every day for the previous week. Then he needed to hear it again. Then he mixed up the order of the questions.

He glared, first at Chantal, then at me. He looked ready to charge both of us with *Looking At Me Funny*, but he just grumbled that he'd have more questions for her later and she shouldn't leave town.

"Excuse me, we're singing in Dallas tomorrow night. I can take responsibility for her, since I'll be onstage with her."

"Are you a singer or a lawyer?" he barked. "Is she an accountant or a singer?"

"Both, for both," I replied. I could tell he wished that were against the law.

Chantal leaned hard against me as we left. I thought about carrying her to the car, but it wouldn't go over well. Even so, Darryl's eyes widened as we staggered through the front door. He ran off to get restorative drinks while we settled in my office's 1940s channel-stitched velvet chairs. The round back is as comforting as an embrace.

I sat in the client chair beside her and took her trembling hand in mine. I held it up as though to take an oath. "Repeat after me: I, Chantal Annette Gaumont, do hereby resolve to never in my entire life do such an idiot thing as creating a fake online identity. I swear this on my next album by the name I hold most sacred."

She withdrew her hand, the better to clutch the other one in her lap. "ABBA?"

"Your choice."

"Are they going to arrest me?

"It would be stupid for them to do so."

"That's no comfort."

"No, but we'll keep investigating."

As he returned with cups of hot tea, Darryl interjected, "The police got a Black girl ready to charge? Yep, you done for, girl."

Chantal dug her fingernails into her hands.

I sighed. "Darryl, without denying the systemic racism and misogynoir in that statement, it's not something you say to clients."

"What's that, *misogynoir*?"

Chantal said in a tight voice, "What they do to you when you're Black *and* female."

Darryl's eyes opened wide. "Double whammy! Only thing worse would be being queer."

Chantal almost spat. "I'm bisexual."

Darryl shook his head in sympathy. "Sorry 'bout that. Been nice knowing you."

I cleared my throat. "Chantal has an advantage that most people don't. Me. That is, legal representation. I see it with my immigration clients. I don't have to be brilliant. I just have to be there. Maybe my client's case isn't any better than anybody else's, but representation makes the difference."

"Also translation and filling out all those forms like I do," Darryl added.

"We couldn't do without you. Chantal, I'll be with you whenever they talk to you, and Darryl's going to fill out all the boring forms I can find, to remind him to watch his mouth when talking to clients and so we don't fall behind on the immigration cases."

Tears welled in Chantal's eyes. "Oh, JD, if I didn't know how full of it you are, I'd be completely moved."

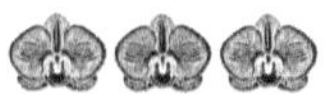

Chantal pressed my hand before tottering to Dianne's office. Her high heels—barely over five feet tall, she always wears heels—clicked on the wooden floor.

Johnny, in contrast, made no noise at all as he entered the room. He leaned against the door jamb while I described our visit with the police.

"You're correct about the IT evidence," he said. "I examined both Chantal's and Mrs. Kelly's computers, and Javonte is coming from a different ISP now. He seems to have reported Chantal's account as the fake one, resulting in its closure."

"So there's another Javonte on the interwebs," I said. "Darryl, does your grandmother go to Javonte's events?"

"She goes to anything that gets her out of the house. Want me to ask her?"

Johnny nodded. "It sounds like the new Javonte has attended the Silver Panther gatherings. He never appears in the official photos posted, though I imagine if you ask around, you'll find someone caught him on camera at some point."

Darryl eyed the stack of immigration forms on my desk. "So I should get photos from my granny and her friends?"

"Priority One," I said.

"Beats cat boxes and government forms," he said as he returned to his desk to get paid for fiddling with his phone.

An inhuman shriek arose from Dianne's office. Johnny returned to his own office at the far end of the house, and I opened my email. Over the years, we'd learned not to panic. Someone might have just stepped in kitten by-products.

Chantal appeared at my office door again. Holding a printout, she glanced from it to me and back.

"I'll give you a spiky style, close on the sides, some color on the ends," she said.

"I think not. I don't spend enough time on stage for such a drastic change."

Chantal was always wanting to make us over for our musical gigs.

"Okay, temporary color," she compromised. "It and the hair goo will wash out, and you can show up in court the next week as boring as ever."

I closed a few tabs on my browser. "Why do I need a makeover?"

She sat in my client's chair and inched forward to confide, "It's Dianne."

"Dianne cares what I look like?"

"She doesn't exactly. I guess I better tell you."

"Yes."

"You know how she pretended to be this Spanish dude to draw her cousin off this guy who robbed her? Her cousin kept getting more intense with Dianne as Diego, and Dianne couldn't keep it up anymore. She killed off Diego and changed his page to a memorial, but then Tía Soledad declared he was the love of her life, and she would do a pilgrimage to his hometown in Spain, going to every place he'd mentioned. And she'd visit his family."

"The imaginary home and family?"

"Right. His nephew or cousin or something—can't remember, but also Dianne—has tried to keep her from going to Spain, but it hasn't worked, and Tía Soledad is talking to travel agents to get the best flights in April."

"You want to dress me up for photos of this young relative?"

"We want you to visit her as this relative and convince her not to go to Spain. She's seen you before, when you were dating Dianne, so we have to make you look different. And more like Diego."

"No."

"It's for Dianne!"

"That's supposed to move me? I warned you two. So did Officer Al."

"JD!"

"No."

"She's crying!"

"Dianne doesn't cry."

"So you see, it's desperate."

"Absolutely not."

An hour later, my curls were purple-tipped and spiky straight. The household agreed I didn't look anything like myself, like that was a good thing.

Dianne's mother had MultiABBA booked for a quinceañera in Dallas the next day, and Dianne wanted me to talk to Tía Soledad on Saturday morning. She typed a letter from Diego and gave me a tiny porcelain trinket box from Spain as Diego's final gift, a pretty glass basket topped with dainty blue flowers, something a grandmother might like. I had a bad feeling about this.

CHAPTER 4

Johnny insisted that we leave for Dallas by noon the next day, before Chantal had finished the sludge she and the rest of her home town of New Orleans call coffee. When she makes the coffee, we know to fill our cups halfway and cut it with water or lots of cream.

Dianne shoved her toward the stairs to get dressed, and Johnny poured the rest of her coffee, both from her cup and the pot, into a thermos mug that would last her the weekend. Because we were taking my Hyundai Sonata, so that I could sit up straight without hitting my head, I started the Tetris-like process of cramming overnight bags and instruments into the car. I laid our yellow satin suits tenderly on top of everything in the trunk in hopes they wouldn't look like used crumpled tissues by the time we took the stage.

Johnny's addition of his crime scene kit raised complaints from one and all. Was he expecting a murder at the quinceañera? He was not, Dianne reminded him, justice of the peace for Dallas County.

He wanted to stop by Nordic Nights, the bar I deduced from the torn business card on Mrs. Kelly's front porch. As a previous performer, I would go in and ask for another gig while Johnny prowled around looking for clues.

"I'm not going in there!" Chantal declared.

I agreed. I had the easy part, asking for a gig I didn't want anyway. Dianne promised Chantal that we'd never sing there again, even if they did want me and my backup band. That phrase sounded good, but I knew I didn't want to be leader of the band. I'd have to expand my repertoire beyond "La la laaaaaaaaaa" and "Does Your Mother Know."

We spent the thirty-minute drive speculating about what the letters meant. The only suggestions were password, acronym, and code. A glance at Dianne told me she was sorry she made that last suggestion, because Johnny then described a book he read about World War II cryptography and the Enigma machine, not something we'd ever wondered about.

Like many downtown bars, Nordic Nights lost its magic in the daytime. It looked like the squat, crumbling warehouses on the next block south, though it did have mostly whole windows. Only one or two had taped cracks.

Because Johnny wanted to go in the back door, I parked on a side street. The door was indeed unlocked, but instead of opening into a dim scene with a few employees preparing for the weekend onslaught, bright lights made us blink. Cops were preparing for a convention, decking the halls with their cheery yellow tape.

Johnny did his signature act of fading into the shadows while law enforcement demanded to know what I thought I was doing and to quit it.

I stepped forward to give Johnny cover in what darkness he could find and stammered that I just stopped by to see the manager about a gig. I added that the door was unlocked.

Officer Friendly was not on duty. His red-faced replacement shouted, "You're in a crime scene. Get out now! Both of you!"

"Could I just use the bathroom?" asked Johnny in his quiet voice as he moved in that direction.

"No! Get out! Lock the door, Schuman. You should have done that before. We'll have every drunk in town stumbling in."

I held up one hand and gobbled like an idiot as I backed up in slow motion to give Johnny time to see whatever he wanted to see. In the other hand I hid my phone, set to video, and rotated it to record most of the room. You never know what you'll catch. Several cops blocked my view of the bar.

Johnny cleared up the mystery when we got back into the car. "Murder. Victim was a slight, mixed-race man, like Darryl, but older. I couldn't tell how old."

"By the bar?" I asked.

He nodded.

"Anybody we know?" asked Dianne from the backseat.

"They gonna blame us?" asked Chantal. "Being suspected of one murder is tiring."

I eased the car back onto Fourth Street, legal in every way, made a nonchalant turn at the light, and proceeded down Fifth Street three miles under the speed limit toward the I-35 underpass. Once on the highway, I put my foot to the floor, not only to get us out of there as fast as possible, but so Austinites traveling even faster wouldn't run me down.

Johnny called Officer Al as soon as we hit the highway. He put it on speaker so I could contribute my bit, but the policeman interrupted his description of the murder scene at Nordic Nights and its possible connection to Mrs. Kelly's death.

"Stop interfering with investigations," he shouted.

"But I always help—"

"Not this time, you don't."

"We didn't give our names, and they threw us out immediately," I said to conciliate.

"JD's there too? I'm telling you, stand back. Stay out of this case. Both cases! All of you! Chantal's still a person of interest in the Kelly murder."

"Hey!" shouted Chantal, wounded. "Johnny and JD cleared me."

Officer Al groaned. "I should have known the whole gang would be here."

"Should have, yes," added Dianne.

Static crackled through his curses. "Look, anything you do will taint the case. Everyone will assume you're pulling tricks to clear Chantal. Keep your distance from the Kelly case, and stay away from Nordic Nights."

Johnny began, "You really ought to look into—"

"I don't want to hear any more from any of you!" The phone went dead.

Johnny wore a frustrated frown. "He's not going to investigate Nordic Nights, is he? It's too much of a coincidence for the cases not to be connected, finding their card twenty miles away in an unrelated neighborhood."

I agreed. "But anything we do will make matters worse."

"You better not be saying 'Trust the system.' Prison's full of people who trusted the system," grumped Chantal.

"We'll do our own investigation when we get back after this weekend, if they're still interested in you," I soothed, or tried to.

I concentrated hard on the road for the rest of the three-hour trip to the Dallas area. That was the only way to escape Chantal's moans about her lost recording session and her fears of being arrested for murder; Johnny's plucking his U-bass, the bass ukulele he prefers when traveling; and Dianne's complaints about my keyboard sticking through the backseat.

The gig went fine—bunch of teenagers hopping around, their parents in the background, munching and matchmaking. The first quinceañera I attended was for Dianne's sister. Dianne—Lupita to her family, short for Guadalupe—prepped me by saying it was like a wedding without the groom. *Nice concept*, I thought.

Shortly after eleven o'clock the next morning, the women were getting mani-pedis at a salon Dianne's sisters liked, I was standing on Soledad Cortez's porch, and Johnny was sitting alone in the car with his phone and laptop. Darryl's grandmother and her friends sent their Silver Panther photos, and he hoped he could pick out the new, in-the-flesh Javonte DeKeyser.

The house looked like all the others in the neighborhood, a product of the 1950s when the soldiers came marching home from World War II, back to their sweethearts and a sweetheart of a GI bill that sent them to college and backed loans for houses. More than half a century later, the war with time showed, but the neighborhood resisted the rot with vinyl siding over the original frame and fresh paint, some too fresh for the average taste. Mrs. Cortez painted her shutters a pinky coral that some might call flamingo. A house at the end of the block was black with lime-green shutters. Another sported purple with lavender trim.

In Diego's cousin's name, Dianne sent her own cousin a message, asking if I could visit. Mrs. Cortez now threw open the door. Her forbidding expression warred with her gracious words of welcome.

The house smelled of lemon polish with undertones of cleaning chemicals, that badge of "I just cleaned my house." I remembered it well from college days, when we were faced with parties or parental visits. Amid the flamethrower in the bathroom, bulldozer clearing the hallways, and clothes shoveled into industrial-sized laundry bags, someone was always wiping lemon polish on the few pieces of splintered wooden furniture.

One time Chantal ran to the store for Pillsbury cookie dough that she whacked into pieces and tossed in the oven. She'd heard that baking cookies created a good impression. Johnny, king of the kitchen even then, took offense that she didn't ask him to create nice-smelling food for the occasion.

Mrs. Cortez didn't go that far. She didn't offer me even a glass of water. I took a deep breath and began my eulogy for Diego and their relationship.

"So you're Diego García Aznar's nephew."

I swallowed. "Cousin is more correct, but I called him uncle."

"Funny. You look a lot like that guy my young cousin Lupita used to date."

Busted. I hoped my purple spiked hair didn't wilt. "When did you know?"

"Weeks ago, when Lupita quoted her own high school graduation speech. Very inspirational."

"You remember her valedictorian speech?"

"No, but I read it to Conchita, her mother." Hurt warred with anger on her face. "Why would Lupita deceive me like that?"

"Because she loves you."

"How can you say such a thing?"

I studied her face, full of pain. "Dia—Lupita took care of all the children in her generation. She did her elders' books and their taxes from the time she was fifteen, so well that your husband asked her to look after your finances. When a situation arose that she couldn't solve with a spreadsheet, she did a dumb thing because she couldn't bear the thought of you being left destitute. In high school, I did more housework and childcare for my twin sisters than my peers, because my mother had cancer, but my life looked like a beach slacker's next to Lupita's responsibilities."

"You should have been happy to help your poor mother!"

"I was, and I would have done another ten years gladly, if only she would have lived."

"But Lupita ran away to college and never came home!"

"She still returns for every holiday and family occasion."

"Not Easter!" declared Soledad in triumph. "Every year her mother cries."

"Lupita's an accountant. She barely sleeps in March and April. The weekend after the tax deadline, she takes the younger sisters and cousins—and my sisters—to buy their prom dresses and summer clothes, like she's done every year since she got her driver's license. She'll take them back in August for school outfits and in November for winter clothes."

Soledad turned away. "I wouldn't know. I had boys."

"By anybody's standards, she's a good daughter, sister, cousin. Being Lupita, she's got to be the best at it. I owe you an apology for my part in this travesty, and I give it freely. Lupita will beg your pardon also, if you give her the chance."

"I am never talking to that girl again. When I think of her laughing at me with her friends—"

"Believe me, she wasn't laughing, though I understand how you might think so. She was trying to keep you away from real predators and give you sound advice at the same time, to get you back into real life."

"He—she told me our love could never be—¡Claro que sí!—that I should go to social events at church, my school, the library, even this thing called Meetup. I promised to go to one activity every week and then I told him—her!—all about it, which I would never have done if I'd known I was talking to Lupita!"

"I hope you'll remember what you said—that she's barely more than a girl, a girl faced with a problem she didn't know how to handle." I rose and reached into my jacket pocket. "You might not want the gift she sent, but you ought to at least see it."

She sniffed as she pulled the trinket box out of its nest of tissue paper. "Something from Diego's family, she wanted me to believe? I suppose it belonged to his mother?" Ladies who work in schools develop serious sarcasm skills.

I winced. "I didn't know the exact provenance, just that he wanted you to have it. It's vintage, not antique, but it is Spanish porcelain."

Sadness swelled her face as she touched the delicate blue roses on top of the porcelain basket. "Pretty." She raised her glistening eyes to mine. "My previous—acquaintance—sent me a message on Thursday. I suppose you'd say he's no more real than Diego?"

"Less, if that's possible. Most likely he's in Ghana, living in a hut whose sole amenity is a speedy internet connection. He—or she—works hard all day, romancing American widows and divorcées out of their money, most of which goes to a syndicate. It's a big industry. You have many sisters." Watching her internal struggles, I added, "Maybe you should keep the basket, to remind you."

She shook her head and stomped over to her computer desk, coyly tucked behind a schefflera plant. "He's in this area. I can show you his emails." She stabbed the keys so hard I expected to see blood on the keyboard. "See, his email is from dfwrr.net."

I hate disillusioning old people. "He could be anywhere in the world and have that address. Let me show you." I took her place at the keyboard and tapped a few times. And then a few more. It did indeed look like a local ISP. "Do you mind if I call in my partner from the car? I know the basics of online spoofing, but he's an expert."

Johnny was polite about it, though he'd have preferred to sit in the car by himself. He needs time to recover after gigs, except for those where the band outnumbers the audience. But his eyes glowed when I showed him the issue. This wasn't a social call, but a problem-solving effort.

"I was sure her correspondent was from Ghana," I said. "But the header looks like a legitimate ISP."

"I see what you mean," said Johnny. "I'll do a quick check." He set his laptop on the desk and drilled his gaze into the screen as he typed.

Mrs. Cortez murmured, "I don't know how you young people learn all these things."

"We grew up on the World Wide Web. And Johnny likes to know how things work."

A smile wobbled on her face. "How do you manage? I didn't realize the dangers."

"Most of us don't have any money, so we don't have to worry about that kind of scam. For personal safety, we worked out systems. If someone was meeting someone for the first time, several others from our house would go to the same place. And the women knew they could call me or Johnny to come get them if they were uncomfortable." I got most of those calls, after Johnny threw Chantal's date through the front door of the restaurant. Johnny, despite his black belts, has trouble gauging the precise amount of force necessary.

Mrs. Cortez looked like she wanted to ask many things, so I turned away from her burning eyes to survey her living room, full of mementos of children now grown, a husband now dead, furniture declined into "serviceable," curtains and carpet with still more wear in them. Making a new acquaintance, even virtually, who kindled all those New Relationship feelings must have made her whole life seem shiny, new, and fascinating.

"Most unusual," said Johnny, interrupting the heavy silence. "This person is approximately three blocks away."

"You see!" she snapped. Her triumph melted into doubt at the speed of microwaved butter. "He told me he lived in Jacksboro and took care of his elderly mother, so he couldn't get away often."

I didn't say anything. She'd already done the math: Garland being on the east side of Dallas and Jacksboro on the west side of Fort Worth added up to a two-hour one-way trip.

"JD and I could investigate for you," offered Johnny. "We could let you know if you want to meet this person."

We could?

We did.

CHAPTER 5

Johnny kept his laptop open and guided me to the address. I hoped and didn't hope that we'd find the scammer attached to a computer.

"Did you find any possible Javontes in the photos?" I asked as a distraction. At the next stop sign, I glanced at him when he didn't answer right away.

"It wasn't hard. Darryl's grandmother circled him in every photo he appeared. No one knew who he really was; they accepted him as Javonte. He apologized for using a different photo online and hoped they'd forgive him. They did, having used younger photos of themselves in the digital world. Since the police don't want us investigating, I sent the photos to *my* grandmother. As a nurse, she helped in medical clinics in three counties. She might have seen him." Johnny spoke in a distracted tone. He wore his data-percolating expression.

"What's wrong?" I asked as I pulled up to the address.

"The murder victim at Nordic Nights looked similar to the fake Javonte, from what I could see." Johnny said, his voice dissatisfied. He likes to be certain. "I checked local news sites, but they haven't posted anything yet."

"And we've been warned off the case, both in Austin and Beauchamp. But at what point are we suppressing evidence?" I frowned, thinking. "After we get done here, I'll check the video I took.

Maybe it will show something besides my fingers. Then we'll send the whole package to Officer Al with my concerns about evidence."

Johnny looked out away, out the window. So did I, scanning the neighborhood. Three blocks away could be halfway around the world in terms of class. From older houses owned by older people who nevertheless worked hard to keep their elderly homes going, like they did for their bodies, we left a thriving neighborhood and entered a random collection of rental houses, smaller and sadder. A house with less than a thousand square feet would squeeze any family larger than two, and nothing screams "rental" like the lack of basic maintenance and repairs. We lived in one of those houses through all our college degrees.

I guessed that many occupants were trying to avoid official attention, like in our old neighborhood. I hoped they all had working toilets.

"What's the plan?" I asked.

Johnny shrugged. "Knock on the door and go with the flow? You're good at that."

"Yeah, that's a plan."

It's what I did, though.

A middle-aged woman who ate fear for breakfast opened the door and shrank at the sight of me. Curtains twitched in the nearby houses. Even with purple hair, I must look like an officer of the court. I tried to infuse comfort in my smile.

"Good morning. I hope I'm not keeping you from church?"

She did look spiffed up, wearing the best Dollar Tree had to offer, maybe not as old as the other things in her closet. She glanced back into the house and shook her head. "We're just getting back."

Seeing teenager detritus in the living room, I made a leap. "Do you know Soledad Cortez? A few blocks over? She's been meaning to come over to ask your son if he'd like to earn money mowing her lawn. I said I'd ask for her."

From the kitchen, a man with a heavy accent answered. With the light behind him, I couldn't make out his features. "My son Chano has a good job with computers."

I gave my name, which led the woman into a reluctant admission that she was Ashley Aguilar. A teenage boy, sporting the latest Converse shoes and better clothes than his mother by several orders of store, stepped in from the hall. "I'm going to the library to do my homework. I can't concentrate with the kids around." The laptop under his arm rivaled mine.

"I could drive you," I said. "You're lucky to have a library open today." I couldn't remember the last time a Texas library was open on Sunday.

He mumbled that I didn't have to do that and the library was closed, but he could work in the courtyard, where it would be quieter.

"I came over to ask if you'd like a job taking care of Mrs. Soledad Cortez's yard. Someone gave her your name. It's a small yard, so it wouldn't take much of your time, but she's getting on in years, and her husband died recently."

The older Aguilars murmured sympathies, but their son's expression looked like Johnny's stray cats when the trap door slams down.

"And on top of that, someone scammed her out of her husband's life insurance, all she had to live on for the rest of her life." I raised my voice over the gasps of horror. "Or maybe you have a friend who could help her. Let's sit on the back porch, and I'll show you photos of the lawn and give you her contact info."

The "back porch" was a euphemism for a slab of concrete. If I laid down on it, my head would be in the dirt, grass being a premium feature. We sat on the one step, Chano perched like it was a razor blade.

"You hardly need her contact info, do you?" I asked. "How much of the $5,000 did you get?"

"Thousand," he muttered.

"Any left?" I looked pointedly at the shoes.

"Not much." He kept darting glances at me, arrows of indecision.

"Did the person or group behind you give you the computer?"

He ducked his head and mumbled, "Yeah. Training and everything. I get enough to pay the internet bill too."

"Nice of them. And of course it's in your mother's name because you're still a minor. Not in your father's name because he's indocumentado."

He couldn't have looked more terrified if I'd held a gun to his head.

"Sir—no—my father—how?—you can't—"

"Let's take it from my side. My partner—" Such an all-purpose word, *partner*. "—is a trustee for her cousin Soledad, known to you as mi vida, cariña, bomboncita, and others. She's older than your mother, but I don't judge. My partner doesn't judge either, not in that way, but she does have feelings about her generous cousin giving away the money her husband left to support her."

He muttered, "They said she could do more."

"She certainly intended to, but her trustee wouldn't approve the funds, not for a roof she didn't need, a fancy car, or a sugar baby. So she went back to work and gave you money from her salary, not controlled by the trustee. My partner was furious, and asked me—did I mention that I'm an attorney?—to file suit against you for fraud. I didn't expect to be able to locate you, but that didn't take fifteen minutes. *Your* partners have left you—and your family—high and dry, vulnerable to anybody who looks. They didn't take the smallest precautions that would have made you look like an overseas account."

"My father could be deported!"

"True, not because anyone's looking for him, but because you helped them find him, and even if he's followed all the rules, he's close enough to a crime to get himself sent back to—"

"Guatemala. He hasn't been there for twenty years! He came here with his family when he was my age!"

"You know exactly how much that will weigh with anybody." I let silence sink hard on us both. "Your father's proud of you."

"What can I do?"

"Can you get out without getting hurt? What if I put parental controls on your laptop? I used to do that for my sisters, and they complained loud and long. If anybody asks, I'm the IT guy that your parents hired to keep their kids away from porn and online predators. I'll do the same for my partner's cousin." He nodded, not wincing. No self-awareness. "You could say your parents are suspicious and watching you harder, so you better give the laptop back and quit the business. Would they let you quit?"

"Maybe? I couldn't do my schoolwork, though."

"That's easier to address. Still, don't go anywhere by yourself for a while."

I'll spare you the technical details of offloading the files he needed for school and fitting his machine with an online chastity belt to keep him out of dangerous places and making sure his email was monitored —by me, from a dummy account. I don't claim it would tie up every kid forever or even for very long. My efforts inspired my sisters to a rudimentary digital education and to a few tech-geek boyfriends. The monitors at least told me when they broke through.

Chano at least had a good cover story. I hoped it would keep him safe.

"What happens now?" he asked, urgent.

"Now you contact your employer and say you've got to give the machine back."

"I mean, what about your partner? What's she going to do?"

It was a good sign that he found Dianne scarier than the goons who hired him. Me too—I'd be more frightened of Dianne than of any villain up to those with nukes. But he didn't know her, so maybe the masterminds weren't that scary. I hoped he was right. If local high-school kids started disappearing, wouldn't the community notice? I stuffed down the whisper that said, "Brown kids, not so much." Dianne's brown family would certainly notice.

I texted Johnny about the upcoming call, in case he could trace it (not that I wanted to know, as an officer of the court). Chano called his employer and explained that his parents were suspicious and had an IT guy put nanny controls on his devices. He explained at length (because I advised him to, to give Johnny longer to trace) that he didn't know how to remove the restrictions and he'd better just quit because his parents thought he was into porn and drugs and he was really in trouble, man.

"I'll give you a ride," I said as we stood.

"Not all the way," he insisted.

Back in the house, he headed to his room while calling to his parents that I was going to drive him to the library so I could meet his friends, who might want to mow Mrs. Cortez's lawn. I smiled in agreement. While the father recited his son's accomplishments, I wondered if I was doing the right thing, taking their kid to meet with a known criminal. The usual "tell the parents" strategy was not going to work, not with a parent in danger of being deported. I vowed I was going to follow much closer than Chano specified. Would that be enough?

He barreled through before I had a chance to finish my Southern departure courtesies. I caught up with him only because he pulled up short when he saw Johnny in the car.

"My partner," I said, glad again for the all-around usefulness of the word. "He's harmless."

Chano shoved something into my hands: legal tender, hundred dollar bills that I couldn't immediately count.

"For—her. If I give something back, will it help?"

"I'll make sure it does," I said. I was sure I could get Dianne to back off from pressing charges. I hoped, anyway.

We headed for downtown Dallas, a long trek from Garland, even though the Dallas metropolis swallowed Garland long ago. A fantastical shiny skyscraper hovered over the nastier parts of downtown. I could have said "unfortunate," but at some point, areas feed on themselves and anyone unwise enough to enter—like seventeen-year-old kids trying to escape a bad situation.

Chano directed us to a restaurant, a red brick building erected far enough in the past to claim "historical," if you liked your history depressing. As Chano sauntered down the street, Johnny kept typing on his laptop until I couldn't stand it anymore. I jumped out and followed the slight figure two blocks ahead of me as he turned left, away from the river. Seconds later another figure zoomed by me and called, "Lock the car."

I stopped to fish my keys from my pocket. I clicked back at the car and cursed Diego's nephew's tight pants as I wiggled my keys back in. I took off after Johnny but stopped at the turning point to rearrange the keys, poking tender places. I couldn't see either Chano or Johnny. The street was vacant, maybe the sad, paint-peeled houses too. I ran toward shouts that rose from a side street a block away.

The area suddenly transformed into rust-level industrial, with a warehouse and its offspring. I caught my breath at the slim, prone figure, sporting the latest Converse. As I ran toward Chano, an unfamiliar body sailed through the air and landed in front of me. As he raised himself to his knees, I pulled him up far enough to punch him in the face and send him down for the count, I hoped.

Johnny, who has more black belts than I can count, was dealing with two other creeps. If you wonder why I didn't go help, I did so once in college, when some gorilla types decided the little Asian kid would be an easy target. Afterwards, as the cops loaded everyone into their cars, he asked me never to do that, unless he was in trouble, because he went into a fight with the attitude of "Today is a good day to die and I'm taking you with me." He didn't want to choke his moves to avoid taking me too.

Besides, somebody needed to check Chano's still, bloody form. I pressed the panic button on my phone as I knelt beside him. Up close, I could hear him moan. Blood still poured from his nose and lips.

Sirens wailed.

I didn't expect the police so soon.

Chano struggled to get up. Not seeing any other injury, I helped him to his feet. We moved at three-legged race speed down a side street. I heard pounding and limping feet behind me and Johnny yelling, "You forgot your laptop." It collided into someone with a thunk. The moan and sound of shattering plastic told me its fate. I wondered if I should stay with Johnny, but surely he had the social skills to tell the cops he was mugged. If not, he must know by now to shut his mouth until I came to bail him out.

Instead he ran flat out to join us seconds later. We made a chair of our arms to carry Chano to the car.

"Shame the computer's broken," I remarked as I pulled onto the tangle of highways over downtown Dallas.

"But Mrs. Cortez is never getting another message from her online wooer," said Johnny with satisfaction.

"Um," came the voice from the backseat.

I glanced in the rear-view mirror, and Johnny turned slightly, favoring his just-worked muscles. Our passenger looked like the horror wasn't over.

"They have all my online cred. They can spoof being me. They're going to clean out her bank account. That's why I had to get in touch with her again after she ghosted me. They told me to get close to her again so they could pull this last thing." His lip bled again with the effort of speech.

Johnny handed him tissues. "That is a shame about the computer then."

"If you want, tell her I'll mow her lawn, for free."

I didn't have to be Dianne to calculate the money involved, but I said I'd pass the word. By the second he reminded me more of my young sisters in trouble.

When we pulled up to the house, I said, "I'm coming in with you. Your parents need to know about your injuries." I raised my voice over the protest. "I'll sanitize the story, but you need to tell them the rest. They'd rather hear it from you than from the cop that knocks on the door. If he knocks."

Johnny added, "We would not—what is the expression?—narc on you. But we cannot control what other people do. Even the police who responded to JD's call might find us." His voice grew reproving. "I am not sure why you did that, JD."

"I thought the guys would flee when they heard the siren, or, if no siren, as soon as the cop car turned on the street. I didn't want you to kill them. That gets awkward for your attorney." I glanced back at Chano, sunk deep in the seat. "Coincidentally, I also practice immigration law. Let's go in, and I'll give your father my card."

I told his parents that after we dropped him off, some guys attacked him and stole his laptop, even though we ran to help.

His mother fussed over him like mothers do but declined my offer to drive them to a doc-in-the-box. Johnny offered his opinion as a veterinarian that Chano seemed okay and didn't hit his head, but of course it was best to consult a human doctor. None of the family wanted to go for medical care, so we had to give it up.

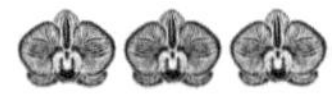

I drove back to Mrs. Cortez's house slower than the speed limit.

Johnny kept busy on his phone. "Ah. My grandmother does know Javonte, or Henry Washington, as she knows him. He's retirement age, but can't afford it, having worked minimum wage jobs all his life. He was doing janitorial work when he came to her clinic. After you check your video, I'll send the information to Officer Al, along with my… suspicions that the Nordic Nights murder victim is Henry." He sounded like he'd tasted something bad. He doesn't like spreading uncertainty. "I don't think Henry Washington could have overpowered a tall, solid woman like Mrs. Kelly, and I wonder where he acquired the skills to hack and steal Javonte's account."

"It's a mystery," I agreed. "But now I'm more worried about what to tell Mrs. Cortez."

"You'll know," Johnny assured me. He has great faith in my verbal skills.

Since I couldn't think of an angle, I just told her the unvarnished truth. I've never seen so many emotions smushed together: humiliation, rage, horror, bewilderment. Those were just the ones I could identify. I handed her Chano's money when I got to the end of the story.

"That's all he had left," I said. "He wasn't allowed to keep much. That's how this business runs: the guys on the bottom take the risks; the guys on top keep the money. He offered to mow your lawn—"

"No!"

I jumped at the explosion.

"I do not ever want to see him. He can mow the church lawn. Father Chinh is always looking for volunteers." With great fury, she scribbled contact info on a square of note paper.

I shoved the note into my pocket; I'd transfer it to my phone later. "Another thing. Though you won't hear from Chano again, you will hear from his overseer, wanting you to clean out your bank account for him."

She picked up her laptop from her desk and handed it to me. "You mean like this?"

"Exactly like that," I said, handing it to Johnny.

The message was heart-rending, a sad story about emergency surgery for someone's mother or pet or something. He couldn't schedule the surgery until he had the money, so would his darling Soledad please, with all haste—

"It's from a different location," said Johnny. "Have you replied?"

"I didn't know what to tell him." She wrung her hands. "He doesn't exist, you said. Or he does exist, but he's a high school boy, younger than my sons."

"It's no longer him. Now it's the adults behind him," said Johnny.

"Whenever there's a question of money, I ask Lupita," I said.

Johnny nodded. "She'll know how to set a trap. She's a forensic accountant."

"Whatever that means!" exclaimed her cousin. "And I don't want her in my house."

"Not even to hear her apology?" I asked. "She feels badly. She did her best to end the situation without causing you pain or embarrassment. I mean, here I am as Diego's nephew." I gestured to my tinted, spiky locks. "Please, Mrs. Cortez. Will you never attend the same family event she does? I don't say you have to embrace her as your beloved niece. What would you think of turning most of the trusteeship over to another person in your family, maybe a man your age or older, someone whose advice you'd respect? I can't see any of my older relatives taking me seriously either. She could still provide financial analysis when needed."

She stared at her lap for a moment before her gaze flickered upwards, hummingbird-fast, to meet my eyes. "I would ask Conchita, Lupita's mother, if I wanted a counselor."

"That's a great idea. I have a lot of respect for her." I hurried on, not wanting to hear that I didn't respect Conchita enough to marry her daughter. "And you all can decide about whether and how to end the trusteeship."

She looked away, chin quivering.

"Lupita always keeps her promises, but this has been a huge burden on her. She knew your husband was asking her to protect you, not just run the numbers and do the taxes."

"How did she know what to say to me? I feel so invaded."

"She's also a single woman who also longs to be appreciated, valued, loved."

"She could get married if she's so lonely!"

I felt like I was sitting on a cactus. "Marriage might include those things; she's determined that it will. She's still kissing frogs, looking for the prince. I know. I'm Frog-in-Chief. I wish it were otherwise, but we both know it's not."

"She'll be here shortly," Johnny interjected, startling both Mrs. Cortez and me.

He'd done his invisibility act. I hadn't noticed him murmuring into his phone by the front door. He put it back in his pocket and joined me on the couch. "If you don't want to see her, we can arrange that, but we have a chance to catch the perpetrator, and Dianne will know what to do." He smiled the polite smile that disarmed most verbal attacks.

CHAPTER 6

The Cortez sisters and cousins dropped off the beautified versions of Dianne and Chantal. Chantal, dancing and bubbling, greeted us with, "The studio had a cancellation on Monday that I can have. Now all I have to do is find some musicians who can show up at three o'clock with me."

"Can you do that?" I asked.

"Maybe. Better than no chance at all. I don't know what I'll pay them with, though." She walked away and started sending texts.

I looked into Dianne's tormented eyes.

She jutted her chin forward, like I've seen in portraits of military leaders. "I can take it, whatever it is." But her lip trembled as I described our day's adventures.

"Come inside and see what Johnny's turned up," I urged.

Her shoulders slumped, but she did, or tried to. Her first step through the door unleashed a torrent from her aunt.

"Lo siento mucho," Dianne said, an apology the first thing out of her mouth.

It gave Tía Soledad pause, and I jumped in the silence to say, "Johnny, show Dianne—Lupita what you've found." I turned to Mrs. Cortez with a smile. "She can unravel this problem."

Dianne turned to her aunt. "Tía, do you know how to contact your credit union on weekends?"

Mrs. Cortez shook her head. Dianne's fingers flew over her phone. "I used to know one of the officers. Most of the family banks there."

She found the name in her contacts and soon had someone on the phone. The conversation in Spanish went too fast for me, but she explained after she hung up that Tía Soledad should write a last email to entrap the criminals. "I'll tell you what to say."

Mrs. Cortez shook her head again. "You write it."

A few minutes later, they sent a message that Soledad would arrange for a transfer in the morning with her credit union, if he would send her his account information.

She received an instant answer that urged her to send the money now. Dianne wrote back that she'd have to be at the credit union itself to send a sum like that. She would do so when they opened in the morning.

We tiptoed out, leaving behind a sullen Mrs. Cortez. I considered inviting her to dinner with us but thought better of it after a glance at her and Dianne's expressions.

For once, Dianne didn't drag us to one of her favorite restaurants in Garland. She voted for Denny's because we could walk there from our hotel; Chantal and Johnny found a nearby Vietnamese restaurant instead. Johnny pronounced it tolerable. I rated it higher than that, but Johnny's grandfather had owned a Vietnamese restaurant.

While we waited for our food, I at last pulled up my video from Nordic Nights. A quick skim told me it was as useless as I expected, all walls and floor, no shots of the victim or anything relevant. Knowing Johnny would want to check for himself, I handed him my phone.

Sure enough, he clicked through frame by frame, ignoring his pho soup. He asked Chantal, "I think there's a sign on the wall. Could you make it readable?"

"Sure," she replied as she disemboweled a spring roll. She says the rice wrapping raises her blood sugar. "I bet it says, 'Employees must wash their hands before returning to work.'"

She gulped a mouthful before working on the image. She learned graphics design so she could make her own promotional materials. It didn't take her long to finish this task, which she called kiddie level.

"Here you go. It says, 'Our Manager Luke Price,' with his photo. So you know who to punch in Saturday night fights."

She held out the phone first to Dianne. When Dianne shrugged it away, Chantal passed it to Johnny, sitting across from her. He shook his head, disappointed, and handed it back to me. I started to stuff it in my pocket, but something made me look harder.

"It's him," I declared, my heart pounding.

"No," Johnny corrected me. "This man is Caucasian. He has a beard and long hair. Henry Washington was biracial with short, grizzled hair and no beard."

"Not Henry, the guy walking down Mrs. Kelly's street the morning she was killed. I thought he was one of the neighbors. What was the manager of an Austin bar doing at a Beauchamp murder scene?"

I punched in Officer Al's phone number. I overrode his initial growl, saying, "I'm helping you with your inquiries. I saw Luke Price, the manager of Nordic Nights, walking in front of Mrs. Kelly's house just before you came out to tag the evidence. I'll upload my evidence, and I'm happy to pick him out of a lineup if you want. Johnny's identified the new Javonte DeKeyser—Henry Washington, who could be the Nordic Nights victim. We'll upload that evidence too."

The policeman didn't answer right away, either taking it in or deciding whether to rip me apart. Then he asked for the address of the bar. I provided it and demanded an update when he'd investigated. He hung up with a grumpy agreement. By the time I sent the video and Johnny sent his photos, both our soups had cooled. Johnny raised his eyebrows at the restaurant owner, who whisked the bowls away and provided new steaming ones. Johnny twitched his mouth into a smile of approval.

"So they're not arresting me?" demanded Chantal.

I grinned. "Officer Al is headed for Austin where he and the Austin police will talk to the Nordic Nights manager. They'll find that you had nothing to do with the murder, besides creating Javonte to begin with."

"Never doing that again," vowed Chantal. "You, Dianne?"

Dianne, hunched against the wall, snarled through her Bánh Giò.

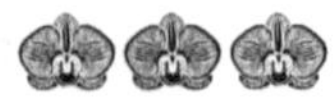

On Monday we took Dianne and her aunt to the tiny credit union. Chantal said she'd stay with them for emotional support.

"We're getting back to Austin by three, aren't we?" she asked as Johnny stepped outside to take a phone call.

"No reason we shouldn't," I said as we followed Johnny. "We'll be gone long before noon."

A slow smile spread over Johnny's normal detached expression. "Officer Al tells me they've arrested Luke Price, the manager of Nordic Nights. He stole Javonte's identity for Henry, the Nordic Nights janitor, who thought his boss was just doing him a favor. Henry joined the Silver Panthers and was awed that this nice, rich Mrs. Kelly took an interest in him. Luke had set up the date in Henry's name that ended in Mrs. Kelly's death. He'd hoped to steal her valuables but ended up with not even one hundred dollars, all she had in the house. Luke had different ideas of wealth than both Henry and Mrs. Kelly. After the murder, Henry confronted Luke, who killed him to preserve his silence. The police in Beauchamp and Austin are investigating other murders and sudden deaths of older women to see if Luke's involved. Officer Al might have apologized too. I couldn't quite understand that part."

"And they don't care about me at all?" Chantal demanded. She sighed in relief that turned to regret. "It's so sad. Henry and Elizabeth Kelly might have been a sweet couple. We could have sung at their wedding."

As we walked back to the car, the credit union being too small for all of us to gather, Johnny said, "Let's drive over to the bank that's supposed to receive the money. I want to see the capture. Aren't the police supposed to pick him up when he shows up for the money?"

The bank was one of the behemoths, not the kind that cared about small change like a six-figure insurance policy. Johnny started to get out of the car, and I put my hand on his arm.

"I want to see who's picking it up," he said.

I cautioned, "The guy I punched yesterday is standing outside the front door. We'll see the others when they come out."

I knew from Dianne that they'd receive a fake receipt, showing they believed they were committing a crime. Sure enough, a short, round man and a taller man emerged not fifteen minutes later, and his henchman fell in behind them.

"Where are the police? Aren't they going to do something?" asked Johnny, already out of the car.

He threw himself at the leader and deflected the henchmen. It's amazing how fast the police showed up then. It took some fast talking, but I got us out of there. I think they thought we'd just complicate things.

When I picked up Chantal's call—her fourth attempt—she said they had taken a rideshare back to Mrs. Cortez's house. She needed to get back to Austin as fast as possible, so we'd better hurry. Mrs. Cortez made sandwiches so we wouldn't have to stop for lunch.

We found Dianne on the front porch swing with her knees pulled up to her chin. With her shoulders hunched, she looked like a tween disappointed in love. I sat beside her while Johnny went inside.

"I am never doing anything for anybody ever again," she said, pressing her forehead on her knees.

"Not even Senior Tax Day at the library?" I asked.

"Nothing," she mumbled. "Nothing for nobody."

"It's not too late for a New Year's Resolution," I observed. February is a schizophrenic month in Texas, teasing with spring temperatures until the trees bud and then shutting everything down with a hard freeze. The last few days had been warm, but the temperature now headed downwards.

"I'm raising my prices for my family. Double."

I draped a tactful arm across the back of the porch swing, maybe brushing her shoulders. "I've been thinking. Johnny and I could do more around the house and the office. You write the grants that bring in the money so we can tilt at windmills. This whole thing works because of you, and it's not right that you be crushed by it while making our lives easy."

She waved an impatient arm. "I'm not crushed. My chore rota runs itself, if everybody keeps their calendar up to date."

"I could do better at that," I admitted, thinking of times she scheduled over my court dates on the Texas border.

She turned her face away, a sure sign of imminent intimate confession. "At home, it was always, 'Let Lupita do it,' and then they'd forget about it because they knew I'd take care of it. But when I say we ought to try for a grant, Johnny dives into the internet and comes back with every statistic recorded on the topic so I can distill it into something meaningful: how much we need, how much that will help the community. Then, for people who don't understand numbers, which is everybody, you write up the text in the most beautiful language that makes me cry every time, because of course that's what I said with the numbers, if only people understood. You make me believe that we're going to save the world if these people toss us a dollar or two. I would so much rather do that than earn even a nickel for a multimillion-dollar firm."

"Me too. I'd much rather save the world. And all the cats, instead of the half that now live with us."

"We've got to get out of here now," Chantal shouted as she barreled out the front door. "Thanks for the sandwiches, Mrs. Cortez. Although I don't know why we're hurrying when I don't have a band. I'll have to do the best I can with what I've already recorded."

Dianne raised her head. "You know you have at least part of a band here, a keyboard and bass, not to mention an alto back up."

Chantal stared at her. "Would you really do that?"

"Of course I would!" said Dianne.

Johnny and I nodded. To keep from laughing at how long Dianne's resolution lasted, I said to Chantal, "I didn't think you wanted us to record with you. You never asked before."

"I didn't think *you* wanted to," said Chantal. "Because of professionalism and all that."

I put my hands on her shoulders. "Chantal, this is Texas. It's a badge of honor to be in a band, especially one with a recording. Even political candidates are proud of their bands. Anybody have a problem with a lack professionalism?"

They didn't. Johnny thought it would make him look more human to his peers.

As we called farewells, Mrs. Cortez came out with a laptop clutched to her chest. "Lupita—" She took a deep breath. "Would you give this to—that young man? Last night I asked my son, the one in IT, if I could have an old computer for…for a deserving high school student in the neighborhood." She held it out, not looking at anyone.

Johnny took it and said he'd set it up on the drive over.

"Tía Soledad." Dianne couldn't quite look at her. "That is generous."

"Don't you ever tell anybody! Not him, not the family."

"I won't! Please, don't you tell anyone about me either. Anyone else, that is." Dianne's face flamed bright red, no doubt thinking that her mother already knew.

"I will tell your mother how brave and clever you were," her aunt promised. "Since she already knows part of the story. And I will show her the lovely porcelain box you gave me as an apology."

Dianne blinked at this creative interpretation. "Oh. Well. Thank you. Maybe she'll speak to me by Christmas."

"Don't like to interrupt this lovefest, but I've got to get to Austin," declared Chantal, pushing Dianne toward the steps. "It's been great, Mrs. Cortez. Glad everything worked out."

Dianne flashed her a grateful look and muttered her good-byes. She and Chantal piled in the backseat, sliding under and around the keyboard and U-bass, the better to work out the playlist. Johnny had the computer set up, complete with the nanny controls, by the time we reached the shabby house. I found Mrs. Aguilar at home and told her that a local nonprofit to help Latino youth had awarded her son a refurbished computer.

The last of our burdens lifted, we argued all the way to Austin about the best songs for our first recording. You know, the important stuff.

If you enjoyed the latest adventures of the Black Orchids, please leave a review at your favorite online bookstore or venue. A review ranks close to a book sale as the best present you can give an author. For gifts and news of the next publications, be sure to sign up for the occasional newsletter and blog post on my website at https://dimond.me.

PLAYLIST AND RESEARCH

Scan the QR code by the chapter title to sing along with the Black Orchids on Spotify (https://spoti.fi/49FDlB2):

- "Thank You for the Music" (ABBA)
- "Move On" (ABBA)
- "Heart and Soul" (Jacques LeGrand)
- "On and On and On" (ABBA)
- "I Have a Dream" (ABBA)
- "Bang a Boomerang" (ABBA)
- "Dancing Queen" (ABBA)
- "My Love, My Life (Benny of ABBA on piano)
- "My Love, My Life" (Amanda Seifert, Lily James, Meryl Streep)
- "I Do, I Do, I Do, I Do" (ABBA)

Though Spotify didn't list it, this version of "My Love, My Life" (ABBA | *Mamma Mia*—Joven, viola; Rommels, piano) is worth a listen. It's similar to what Johnny and JD played.

https://bit.ly/ViolaLy

AFRICAN FABRIC

If you'd like to find fabrics from Africa like Doria Langston wore, check out Miriam Galadima-Benson's fabric store.

https://quiltafricafabrics.com

TEXAS MUMS

Early readers had no idea what Texas homecoming mums were. Homecoming mums have grown from a single chrysanthemum corsage to...hard to describe. In the 1930s, you pinned your mum to your dress with a long, straight pin. Later, it hung around your neck. Now, you wear a harness to hold it up at homecoming day and night activities. Let me provide pictures, always worth at least 1000 words each.

https://bit.ly/MumZine
https://bit.ly/mumsTX

Even businesses like Whataburger, a beloved Texas hamburger chain, get involved, providing mums made from supplies in the store.

https://bit.ly/BurgerMums

ABOUT THE AUTHOR

After stints in professional orchestras, law firms, cat rescue, bookkeeping, and technical communication, M. R. Dimond returned to a childhood dream of writing fiction, which has turned out to be about musicians, lawyers, veterinarians, accountants, and cats.

Sign up for the newsletter to learn about the next Black Orchid Enterprises mystery, or see some previous works:

- *Birth of the Black Orchids*, Black Orchid Enterprises Mystery Book 1
- *The Sphynx Who Stole Christmas*, Black Orchid Enterprises Mystery Book 2
- *Family Matters*, Black Orchid Enterprises Mystery Book 3
- "Playing It Again" in *Hook, Line, and Sinker*, Seventh Guppy Anthology, edited by Emily P. W. Murphy
- "Be It Resolved" in *Riddles, Resolutions, and Revenge*, R. B. Marshall, collator
- "Blessed" in *Dreaming the Goddess*, Karen Dales, editor
- "Nine Lives Through Time" in *Cat Tails, War Zone*, Rebecca McFarland Kyle and Dana Bell, editors
- "Carol for Mixed Voices" in *Best of Strange Horizons Year 2*

Find me on Facebook as Madeleine.Dimond and Instagram as MRDimondAuthor.

9 781956 204131